"WOMAN, YOU DID THAT ON PURPOSE!"

"I'm so very sorry," she said.

She never got to finish her apology, as Lucien reached up to haul Lady Penelope unceremoniously across his stomach, her startled face now only inches from his own. Staring at her meaningfully, he could see the indecision in her eyes and delighted in the way her gaze flitted nervously away from his, moving down to his slightly open mouth.

"Come here, little puss," he breathed softly, his mouth now hovering a scant inch above hers. "Let me hear you purr."

Then his lips were on hers and the time for thinking was over . . .

Avon Books are available at special quantity discounts for bulk purchases for sales promotions, premiums, fund raising or educational use. Special books, or book excerpts, can also be created to fit specific needs.

For details write or telephone the office of the Director of Special Markets, Avon Books, Dept. FP, 105 Madison Avenue, New York, New York 10016, 212-481-5653.

THE PLAYFUL LADY PENELOPE

KASEY MICHAELS

AVON BOOKS ◆ NEW YORK

THE PLAYFUL LADY PENELOPE is an original publication of Avon Books. This work has never before appeared in book form. This work is a novel. Any similarity to actual persons or events is purely coincidental.

AVON BOOKS
A division of
The Hearst Corporation
105 Madison Avenue
New York, New York 10016

First Avon Books Printing: September 1988

AVON TRADEMARK REG. U.S. PAT. OFF. AND IN OTHER COUNTRIES, MARCA REGISTRADA, HECHO EN U.S.A.

Printed in the U.S.A.

K-R 10 9 8 7 6 5 4 3 2 1

Chapter One

IT WAS one of those rare, warm November days that rudely mocks the approaching winter, while setting young hearts stirring with a longing to search out the romantic atmosphere—or perhaps a smidgeon of the adventurous enterprise—of the summer just past.

Indeed, this late autumn phenomenon may have explained the painfully thin, noticeably balding, Assistant Vicar Archibald Wilkinson's invitation to the past-her-first-blush Miss Abigail Pettibone to take a stroll through the spinney on the edge of Weybridge Manor in order to admire the "delightfully colored phyllome."

It certainly had everything to do with Miss Pettibone's precipitant acceptance of the man's offer (for, even if she didn't have the faintest idea what phyllome was, she was certainly able to sniff out opportunity well enough when it came rapping at her door).

As for the youthful hearts' longing for adventurous exploit? Ah, they had been happily roaming abroad since just after breakfast, and were at that very moment already heading straight for the spinney.

"What a delightful suggestion that was, as are all your suggestions," Miss Pettibone complimented her companion an hour later, patting the empty place beside her invitingly as she sat down on one edge of the depressingly cool stone bench that had been placed in the clearing, which had once boasted a peasant cottage but now held only a few lichen-covered leaning brick walls and a decrepit, abandoned dry well.

Her fingers nervously twirling the stems of the bouquet of multihued leaves she and her shy swain had gathered on their walk, she kept her eyes demurely on the rapidly crumbling foliage while her mind did handsprings as she attempted to conjure up a way to maneuver the dear man into declaring himself. After all, Abigail was three and forty, and the time for subtlety was long since past.

"It's gone three," Mr. Wilkinson informed her sadly as he repocketed his watch. "The Vicar will soon be wanting his tea. Perhaps we should start back? The Vicar doesn't like for me to keep him waiting."

"Oh, do sit down, Archie, and admire the view with me," the desperate woman fairly ordered, sweeping off her woefully out-of-date straw chip bonnet to reveal what she privately believed to be her best feature—a full head of coal black hair which hid not so much as a single strand of grey within the confines of its tight bun. "I vow, I do believe this particular site holds one of the most pleasant vistas on the Marquess's entire estate."

As Archibald dropped ungracefully onto the bench, stunned by his companion's familiar use of his name, Abigail began lightly fanning herself with her bonnet, encouraging the aroma of her generously applied homemade lavender and rosewater to waft gently in his direction.

The Assistant Vicar abruptly sneezed into his large white handkerchief and noisily blew his nose, actions for which he then profusely apologized and which Abigail—being of all things a lady—tactfully ignored.

"I have heard it said that this old well grants wishes to those who drop a pennypiece inside it," Abigail said, batting her stubby eyelashes at her companion, who fortunately stopped himself from asking if the poor lady had somehow got some smut in her eye and only looked at her inquiringly. "Of course it is only hearsay, you understand, and applicable only for . . . well, never mind," she trailed off coyly, getting up to walk over to the crumbling stone well.

But Mr. Wilkinson had not resided in the neighborhood for twelve years without hearing tales about the powers of the well himself, and some long-suppressed imp of mischief struggled to the surface, making him say, "The magic works only for lovers, I believe, Miss Petti—*Abigail*." Rising hesitantly to his feet, he walked over to join the woman now leaning over the side of the well, her left foot thrust out behind her for balance (thereby displaying a good three inches of bony ankle). Putting his head to within an inch of hers he was emboldened to say, "I believe I have a pennypiece in my pocket, if you care to make a wish."

"D-do you think the well would grant my wish?" Miss Pettibone breathed, knowing she was within ames-ace of getting the man to declare himself.

The Assistant Vicar swallowed hard before speaking— his prominent Adam's apple working visibly in his throat— blissfully unaware that the impish spirit of "adventurous enterprise" was about to bully its way into this romantic, bucolic setting. "Abigail, I—"

"Archibald Wilkinson . . . consider well what you do!"

"Who-who said that?" Wilkinson quavered, looking about wildly at the surrounding, overhanging trees.

The deep, portentous, disembodied voice came again, this time saying, *"I am the Spirit of the Well, who knows all . . . sees all . . . tells all. Hear me and mark my words. Beware, Assistant Vicar Wilkinson. Beware the wiles of desperate women!"*

Archibald, a poverty-stricken second son who had embraced the church some twenty years earlier through necessity and not through any real vocation, immediately made the superstitious, lower-class sign against the evil eye as he backed slowly away from the well, babbling something that sounded much like, "Away, Satan, I renounce you," while Miss Pettibone, who was made of sterner (and decidedly more suspicious) stuff, narrowed her eyelids and peered intently into the darkness at the bottom of the weed-choked dry well.

"Who is that? Who's down there?" she challenged, the force of her shrilly voiced question hitting against the dank stones that lined the hole and sending back the mocking echo: *"There? . . . there? . . . there?"* Reaching out one hand, she detained the about-to-flee Assistant Vicar quite simply by grabbing a firm fistful of the man's coattail and hauling him back as if he were a particularly recalcitrant fish trying to elude the hook. "I repeat—who's down there? How dare you eavesdrop on our private conversation?"

"Miss Pettibone," Archibald interrupted nervously, "do you really think it is wise to antagonize the Spirit? I mean—"

"Shut up, you fool!" Miss Pettibone commanded testily, her anger at seeing her plans (and her eau de toilette) all gone for nothing, her chagrin at being thwarted in this—surely her last—bid for matrimony overriding her good sense and allowing her quarry to see a side of her that she had hoped to keep firmly hidden until after the ceremony. "Any idiot knows there's no such thing as a Spirit of the Well. It's one of those horrid Rayburn brats, I'm sure of it."

The acrobatic Adam's apple performed once more as Archibald tried to digest this last distressing bit of information on top of everything else that had occurred in the past few moments—not the least of which being the rapidly dawning realization that he, thanks to whomever or whatever was at the bottom of the well, might at this very moment be experiencing what could only be called a "lucky escape."

"One of the Marquess's young sons?" he squeaked in horror, conjuring up a mental picture of Lords Cosmo and Cyril Rayburn, the totally irreverent, irresponsible twin terrors who had constituted two of the many banes of the Assistant Vicar's existence ever since they had released a particularly odoriferous badger into the midst of his first formal meeting with the Friends of the Congregation Ladies Guild many years earlier. "But they're away at school, I'm sure."

"Not anymore they're not," Miss Pettibone answered shortly, releasing her grip on Wilkinson's coattails now that she had his attention once more. "They were sent down last week for starting a fire in their rooms—to toast bread, as I've heard it told. Nearly burnt down the whole building."

Leaning forward even further in order to see into the well, she then commanded Archibald to take hold of her waist as she cupped her hands to her mouth and yelled into the depths, "Lords or no, I'll have your father take the birch rod to you if you don't come up here this minute. Do you hear me?"

4

"Hear me? . . . hear me? . . . hear me? . . ." was the only answer that came up from the bottom of the well, and Miss Pettibone, who knew a fruitless exercise when she confronted it, allowed herself to be drawn back away from the yawning hole before her righteous anger could get the better of her and talk her into muttering something she would rather not have come back at her in the form of an accusatory echo.

Then, winking broadly at the Assistant Vicar as she pushed her badly listing bun back on top of her head, she said loudly, "If they refuse to step forward and take their punishment like men, I do believe we have no option but to cut the rope holding this huge bucket so that the twin hidden somewhere out there in the spinney cannot lower it down to rescue the twin playing pranks at the bottom of the well. What say you, Mr. Wilkinson?"

"Cut the rope? But, Miss Pettibone, consider—it's as thick around as my wrist. However would—"

At this display of faintheartedness, Miss Pettibone pulled a disparaging face that would have banished any thought of offering to share the rest of his life with her (if, indeed, any such consideration remained within Archibald's thin breast), although her expression did cause him to subside into red-faced silence as he realized that she—crafty female that she was—had only been throwing out a dare, hoping that the twins would confess in order to stop her from cutting the rope.

However, just as the Assistant Vicar—no longer the loverlike swain but now the awed admirer of the woman's shrewdness—was about to congratulate her, there came the rustling of dry leaves from the far side of the clearing and two impeccably dressed young exquisites emerged from the trees, lightly swinging their highly polished malacca canes as they sauntered indolently into the sunlight, twin pictures of Innocence Abroad In The Country.

"What ho?" one of the handsome blonde youngsters exclaimed, stopping in his tracks to raise his cane and point it in the general direction of the well. "What have we here, brother? Have we by chance stumbled upon a lovers' tryst? Dear me, how terribly gauche. I do believe we are decidedly *de trop*, don't you?"

"Nonsense, brother," drawled the other, lifting a rather gaudy gilt-edged quizzing glass to his eye to peer interestedly down the length of his elegantly aristocratic nose at the two irate people. "It is only dear Mr. Wilkinson and the Spinster Pettibone. Nary a dropperful of romance to be found betwixt the two of them, or my name ain't— Oh, dear, who exactly am I, anyway? It escapes me at the moment. Am I Cosmo, or am I Cyril? Sometimes methinks we should have our tailor sew our names in our coats, don't you?"

It was true, of course, that the twins were as alike as two peas in a pod, a happy coincidence of birth that had been employed to good advantage by the pair ever since they were old enough to discover the absolutely delicious havoc their unique alikeness could cause to nurses, governesses, teachers, and anyone else who had the misfortune to come upon them when they were of a mind to frolic—which was the same as to say, anyone who chanced upon them during any of the twins' waking hours.

Nodding to acknowledge his brother's question, the first twin magnanimously supplied the missing information. "I ate the kippers this morning at breakfast as I recall, and as Cyril cannot abide the delectable things, it can only mean that you, my dear chap, are he. As it works out, that only leaves me to be Cosmo, which is fortunate as Cosmo is the elder by twelve minutes and, or so I've heard, the possessor of much the superior intellect of the two. Isn't that right, Mr. Wilkinson?"

"What—what's that?" the Assistant Vicar asked, as he had been momentarily distracted by what he was sure was the sound of gnashing teeth, which he had heard coming from the vicinity of Miss Abigail Pettibone.

"Never mind all that, Archy," Miss Pettibone said irritably, waving her hand to silence the man as she glared at the Rayburns. "You think you're so smart, don't you?" she sniped, her upper lip curling as she spoke.

Cosmo turned to Cyril, one finely arched brow raised a fraction. "We do? Oh, I don't know about that. I think I'm fairly well furnished in my upper rooms, but I can't go so far as to say I'm actually *bookish* or anything.

Brother, have you been boasting about your brainbox? I consider that to be excessively shabby of you, really I do."

"*Moi?*" Cyril exclaimed in shocked accents, one hand to his breast. "*C'est exécrable! C'est abominable!* That you, my brother—flesh of my flesh—could suggest such a thing. I have never been one to flaunt my superiority. Indeed, my humbleness in the face of my overwhelming brilliance is one of my most outstanding attributes."

Archibald Wilkinson knew defeat when it jumped up and smacked him in the face. Taking Miss Pettibone by the elbow, he said gloomily, "The hour grows late. I think we should be going, don't you?"

"No, I don't!" Abigail spat, clearly not ready to abandon the field, leaving the victory to the obnoxious Rayburns. "They may have hoodwinked you, Mr. Wilkinson, walking in here acting as innocent as you please, but I know better. I cut *my* wisdoms a long time ago!"

"Two score years or more, I'd say, wouldn't you, brother?" Cosmo asked his twin sotto voce.

"But, Miss Pettibone," Archibald insisted, tugging on her arm as the woman began showing signs of a person seriously contemplating mayhem, "they couldn't have been in the well a few minutes ago and be here with us now. I believe you must be overwrought."

"In the well, you say?" Cyril asked, walking over to peer down into the empty darkness. "Whatever would we be doing in the well? Dashed filthy place to be. You two been nipping at the wine our father sent over to the Vicar last week? Tsk, tsk. For shame, Mr. Wilkinson, employing strong spirits to weaken the resolve of this virtuous lady."

Cosmo, who had joined his twin beside the well, extracted a pennypiece from his pocket and tossed it lightly into the opening. "Speak, O Spirit of the Well," he intoned solemnly, folding his hands together as if in an entreaty. "Reveal yourself to us so that we may beg a wish of you."

"Nothing's going to happen now, you ridiculous man," Miss Pettibone scoffed as the Assistant Vicar took three quick steps backward away from the well. "It's all a trick, I tell you. There's no spirit down there—just some smelly

7

puddles and weeds. I don't know how they did it, but these two rascals are hoaxing you."

"Who dares question my existence?" came the disembodied growl from the depths of the well, the eerie voice succeeding at last in convincing Miss Pettibone and Mr. Wilkinson of the advisability of vacating the premises before the Spirit took it upon itself to turn nasty. The two—one a true believer, the other a recent but ardent convert—their eyes wide with fear, beat a hasty retreat from the clearing as the smiling Rayburn twins took out large white handkerchiefs and gaily waved the pair on their way.

"Good show, Spirit, and all that," Cosmo congratulated, peering down into the well.

"Answer me or know my wrath! I said—who dares question my existence?" the spirit, obviously enjoying itself immensely, commanded dangerously before the sound of some very unthreatening giggles rose to the top of the well.

"I dare!" growled a deep male voice, causing the twins to whirl about sharply in the direction from which the sound emanated, their appreciative smiles effectively banished.

"Papa!" they exclaimed in unison, stepping smartly apart as the tall, powerfully built man approached, his heavy walking boots crushing the dry leaves into the soft dirt as they strode purposefully toward the well.

"Cosmo . . . Cyril," the Marquess of Weybridge acknowledged, his steely gaze slicing to one of his sons, then to the other. "I have been amusing myself for some moments, watching you bait that simpleton Wilkinson and the Medusa Pettibone, but now there is something about this enchanted well that intrigues me more than watching you enjoy yourselves with yet another juvenile prank. Give me a pennypiece, Cosmo. I wish to ask a question of my own."

"Er, um, I don't think I have another pennypiece, Papa," Cosmo stalled lamely. "And like you said, it was just a juvenile prank, and over now. My goodness, look at the time! The sun's nearly below the trees. Perhaps another time we'll all come back here, and we'll show you how the trick was done. Isn't that right, brother? We'll just go on home now and—''

"A coin. Now!''

Cosmo began a frantic search of his person, at last unearthing the single gold piece remaining from his quarterly allowance. "All I have is this sovereign, Papa,'' he said, displaying it in his outstretched palm.

"I'll take it,'' the Marquess said, and did.

"But—but, sir,'' Cosmo whined as the coin exchanged owners. Suddenly he looked his tender age of twenty, all sophistication stripped away as he contemplated the gravity of his loss. "Couldn't you just ask Cyril here for a pennypiece? After all—''

"A capital idea, son,'' Philo Rayburn agreed, turning to hold out one beefy hand to his other son. "I like the idea of feeding only gold to our Spirit, however, Cyril.''

"Yes, sir,'' Cyril acknowledged fatalistically as a second gold sovereign joined the first in the Marquess's palm. "But she'd better catch 'em.''

Upon hearing this slip of the tongue, the Marquess lifted his unencumbered hand and rubbed it wearily against his mouth. "The Spirit is a 'she'? I have to admit it. Until this moment I had held out some faint hope that—*You stay right there!*'' he warned severely as the twins looked about to bolt.

"Spirit of the Well,'' he called out loudly, dropping the coins one by one down into the darkness. "I come begging not a wish, but a small piece of wisdom to guide a father who is old and tired and sorely tried. What punishment do you think fitting for a willful daughter who defies her father and plays hoydenish pranks like some silly schoolgirl when she should be married, with children of her own?''

"*A young woman who refuses the ridiculous shackles of marriage is a treasure beyond price. Guard her well and reward her for her wisdom,*'' the Spirit of the Well immediately answered defiantly.

Cyril shook his head in amazement. "Pluck to the backbone, I'll say that for her,'' he said in admiration.

"You would,'' his father shot back resignedly, his naturally ruddy complexion taking on a dangerously purple hue. "Now put your backs to it, boys, and hoist that impertinent chit out of there before I'm tempted to cut the rope myself and leave her there to grow moss!"

Cosmo was already reaching for the gnarled wooden handle that would lower the bucket into the well. "Penny!" he called out as the Marquess whirled on his heel and strode away. "The jig is up. Get ready to grab the bucket."

"And tell her to clean herself up and present herself to me in the Athenian Room in one hour," Philo Rayburn tossed back over his shoulder as he neared the end of the clearing. "I'd tell her myself, but I might throttle her if I have to look at the idiot child squatting in a bucket like some half-drowned piglet pulled from the bog."

"Yes, sir," Cyril answered smartly, guiding the bucket as it descended slowly into the darkness. "It was all our idea anyway, sir," he rushed to admit. "We saw the Assistant Vicar and Miss Pettibone, and thought it would be the grandest good fun to hoax them. Cosmo and I—we're the ones talked Penny into it, sir."

"That blatant lie will cost you one week of riding your new hunter, Cyril," the Marquess replied tonelessly. "This prank has Penelope's stamp all over it."

"He's got you there," Cosmo admitted as their father's figure disappeared into the trees. "It was Penny who suggested we lower her down the well. You wanted to put our handkerchiefs over our faces and pretend we were low toby men come to rob them, remember?"

The creaking of the wooden handle muffled the sound of Cyril's colorful reply, and soon the large oaken bucket was returned to the surface, carrying its slight burden.

First to appear was a glorious profusion of heavy, burnished gold hair that fell in loose curls down to the tiny, sprigged muslin enclosed waist that was visible above the rim of the bucket. Daintily formed hands and slim, white arms were extended above the small head, their length twined tightly around the thick rope for balance as the twins hoisted the bucket to the top of the stone wall and secured it safely.

After looking around and assuring herself that she was not in danger of tumbling back down into the well—which she had been unhappy to learn was densely populated with slimy frogs, long-legged spiders, and various other small, unlovely specimens—she turned to smile widely at her partners in crime.

It was a pixie's face that Cyril and Cosmo saw, a small, triangular face that housed softly curved, generous lips; a pert, *retroussé* nose; and huge, wide green eyes that boasted an overabundance of long, sooty lashes beneath equally dark, winglike brows.

The twins, however, remained unimpressed by all this beauty as they had seen it all before and considered their only sister to be no more than passably pretty, not to mention the fact that the face they were looking at was streaked all over with brown and green dirt, the hair that seemed to be everywhere was tangled, darkly damp in spots, stuck here and there with twigs, rotted leaves, and—

"Hold on a moment, Penny," Cosmo warned. "You've got a soothsayer in your hair."

"Eeeek! Where? Oh, Cosmo, get it out, do!"

"I said hold still, blast it!" her brother yelled, trying vainly to extract the large, grass-green mantis without injuring it. "Heaven only knows how many bugs this creature has already nipped out of your hair. You should be grateful, Penny, not trying to swat it like it was some stupid insect. Got it," he then exclaimed triumphantly, setting the large insect down a safe distance from his sister's foot and watching while the soothsayer assumed its usual, prayerful position.

"It is a stupid insect, you fool," his sister responded, bending over to scrub at her hair, just to be sure there were no other unwelcome guests taking up residence without her permission. "If it was intelligent, it wouldn't have tried to nest in my hair."

Pushing her splayed hands against her brow at her hairline, she stood upright, tossing her long locks back as she rose and allowing them to tumble down past her shoulders in a reddish gold mantle. "There," she stated, once more in control. "Everything's all right and tight again."

"Only a female could say anything so ridiculous with such conviction," Cyril, who had been silently observing the goings-on, said quietly. "Here, Penny," he added, offering his handkerchief. "You can scrub the worst of the muck off your face with this, but Doreen will skin you alive when she sees that gown. You look like someone put you away wet, and you've gone to mildew. Now hurry! Papa expects you to present yourself in the Athenian Room in an hour."

Lady Penelope Rayburn stopped in the midst of brushing down her gown with her hands to look up at her brothers. "The Athenian Room? My, how formal. A bit out of curl, is he? Do you think he'll cut up stiff about our little prank? Really, it was all quite harmless. Besides, we saved poor Archibald from a fate worse than death. That should mean something."

Cyril motioned for his sister to precede him along the well-traveled shortcut that ended at the bottom edge of the West Prospect of Weybridge Manor, saying, "You know full well that Papa enjoyed every moment of our prank—until he realized that, with Cosmo and I both visible, *you* were the only logical person to be playing Spirit of the Well. You're nineteen now, Penny, and he expects you to start behaving like a lady. Lord, I still can't understand how Cosmo and I let you talk us into lowering you down in that bucket. I'm just lucky that all I lost was my hunter."

"Don't forget our blunt," Cosmo put in as he brought up the rear of their little expedition.

"Oh! I forgot!" their sister exclaimed, dropping at once to the ground in the middle of the path and removing her right jean half boot, shaking it so that two shiny golden sovereigns tumbled into the dirt. "I put them there for safekeeping. And don't worry about Nemo, Cyril. I'll be happy to exercise him for you."

"If she can sit down," Cosmo muttered under his breath. Louder he said, "When Papa gets through with you, sister mine, you may be eating your mutton from the mantel."

Springing lightly to her feet once more, Lady Penelope began skipping down the path ahead of the twins. "Oh, pooh, Cosmo," she scoffed, dismissing his words. "Don't be such a gloom and doom merchant. You too, Cyril. You know Papa is more than used to our little pranks. He's just playing the Stern Parent right now. It will soon suit him to be amused by this day's work. You'll see. Besides, I've never yet seen the day that I couldn't bring him 'round to my way of thinking. It's because I remind him so of Mama, you know.''

The twins exchanged knowing glances, shaking their blonde heads. ''Not this time, infant,'' Cosmo prophesied darkly. ''You may have heard Papa's voice, but you didn't see his face. You've tried him once too often. This time I think he's going to demand your obedience.''

''In what way, O wise one?'' his sister asked, holding out her skirts as she tippytoed around a slight puddle in the narrow path.

''By becoming who you were meant to be,'' Cyril pronounced fatefully. ''By being Lady Penelope Rayburn— and by agreeing to a Season in London's Marriage Mart.''

''Never!'' Lady Penelope declared fiercely. ''Papa knows I shall never agree to any such thing!''

The twins, once again assuming the studious nonchalance of the recently sophisticated, tucked their canes under their arms and replied as one: ''Who says he is going to ask for your agreement?''

Chapter Two

THE Athenian Room at Weybridge Manor was the most formal of the many Rayburn drawing rooms, having been fitted out in the finest Grecian style by the current Marquess's late father during the heyday of the Dilettanti Society, his selections guided by Stuart's *Antiquities of Athens* (the fine eighteenth-century publication that later exerted such a lamentable influence on one period of Sheraton's work).

Precisely spaced niches curved along the gleaming, white stucco walls, each recessed area housing its own marble bust of some long-dead Greek, while the great length of the room was cleverly broken up by the strategic placement of a dozen graceful Doric columns that supplied little by way of structural support, but had served the twins and their sister well in their younger days as they played their own bizarre version of the Maypole dance by tying multicolored streamers about the columns and swinging from them like the monkeys pictured in one of their lesson books.

Ordinarily, the Athenian Room was one of Lady Penelope's favorite places, as it was light, sunny, and rarely visited by the servants—who vowed all those empty marble eyes were watching them as they went about their business—but she found herself curiously reluctant to enter the room this day. Opening the door to no more than a wide crack, she then peered around it hesitantly in an attempt to sniff out the atmosphere before admitting to her presence.

The opening of the hallway door, however, had served to set up a crosscurrent of air, which sent the filmy white, floor-to-ceiling draperies that hung on either side of the many French doors to dancing, alerting the Marquess to his only daughter's presence. "If you were planning a sneak attack, child," he said in his usual deep, rumbling tone, "I'd suggest you drop back and rethink your strategy."

Lady Penelope immediately straightened to her full, unimposing height, flung the double doors open wide, and marched herself smartly into the very center of the room. "There is nothing remotely covert about my entrance, Papa, as you can see," she announced in her soft, faintly husky voice. "However, when this interview is concluded, I do beg you to disregard the rather large wooden horse I have been forced to leave behind me in the hallway. I miscalculated in its construction, I fear, and it wouldn't fit beneath the archway."

"There is a fine line between keen wit and cheekiness," Philo Rayburn pointed out wearily, lowering himself heavily onto one of the low, upholstered couches that were scattered about the room, "and you, my girl, have succeeded in passing over that boundary twice in as many hours. The time has long passed for you to play the hoyden. I have been giving your future a great deal of thought, as you already know, and your latest exploit has only reinforced my resolve to have you settled. Now sit yourself down and listen to what I have to say."

"Oh, pooh, you are going to lecture me." Lady Penelope pouted, taking in her sire's stern expression. Hurrying over to fling herself down in his strong lap and then wrapping her slim, bare arms around his neck, she rested her head against his chest and looked soulfully up into his eyes. "Poor darling, I have upset you terribly, haven't I? You know how dreadfully sorry I am, Papa, and I promise not to go down that filthy old well ever again. It was prodigiously dark, you know, and I was frightened right down to my toes. I can't imagine what possessed me to believe that I should like to try such a stunt, although perhaps this particular prank could be classified under the heading of 'Good Works,' as it did save silly Mr. Wilkinson from falling into the clutches of that horrid Abigail Pettibone."

As she spoke, Lady Penelope rubbed her head against the Marquess's shoulder like a kitten who craves a soft scratching behind its ear, her unbound hair warming his neck and chin as he saw the very image of his wife reflected in the deep, emerald pools of her wide, innocent eyes. Almost, he relented, for he had thoroughly enjoyed the spectacle of the shrewish Abigail Pettibone in full retreat.

But it was that same disquieting image of his wife that provided the necessary starch to his backbone and prompted him to push his daughter away from him, saying resolutely, "Batting those absurd eyelashes won't cut any wheedle with me, child. It may have before, but not this time."

"Why, Papa," his daughter exclaimed innocently, eyelashes in full flutter, "whatever do you mean?"

"I mean," he said, closing his own eyes against the pitiful sight of his youngest child's trembling, full lower lip and threatening tears, "that this day's prank is the last I will tolerate from you, Penelope. I admit to looking the other way when all of you were younger, knowing that Philippos and the twins exerted their influence on you—older brothers will do that, I fear, especially with no softening motherly influence around to guide you. But now, with Philippos riotously living his own life up in London, and those scamps Cosmo and Cyril away at school for the most part, it has gradually dawned on me that you, my precious daughter, have taken over the role of instigator with a vengeance."

"But, Papa—"

"Don't interrupt me when I am trying to make a point!" the Marquess ordered. "To continue: it was *you* who stuffed up poor Isobel Frampton's ear trumpet with wax at choir rehearsal so that the old dragon thought she had gone stone deaf; *you* who ordered that ridiculous feathered hatchment put up on the Farmer Watley's henhouse when the idiot's favorite old rooster was run down in the roadway by the mail coach; *you* who spread that ridiculous farradiddle last year about a sea monster gobbling up all the geese in the village pond; *you* who—"

"Yes, but, Papa—"

"Oh, I might have laughed along with everyone else at the time," Philo went on, waving away her protests, "but you've passed your nineteenth birthday, and it is more than time now for you to put a period to these childish pranks. You must learn to comport yourself like a young woman of birth and consequence. I still can't remember exactly how you talked me out of presenting you this past Season, but mark my words, missy, you'll not bring me 'round your thumb this time. My mind is made up. You are to resign yourself to it—we leave for London the first week of the new year to prepare for your debut.''

Upon hearing this pronouncement, the young ''woman'' in question hopped to her feet in high dudgeon, flounced over to stand in front of one of the French doors, then whirled around to confront her father. ''How utterly ridiculous! All this fuss and pother over a silly Pettibone! Well, I won't have it, do you hear me? I won't! I am not some bit of blooded cattle to be groomed and polished and sold to the highest bidder. Besides,'' she sniffed confidently, ''I defy you to find any male in the whole of England who is courageous enough to take me on once I've made it known that _I_, Lady Penelope Rayburn, bow to no man.''

Lady Penelope in the role of clinging infant was hard to resist, but Lady Penelope in a rage was a sight to melt the coldest heart. The living curtain of golden red hair that shimmered in the sunlight as it spilled around her face and fell in loose curls nearly to her elbows, throwing a soft halo of light all about her upper body; the petite, well-formed, pale green muslin clad frame that seemed so oddly vulnerable in its attitude of defiance; the flashing emerald eyes, flushed cheeks, and defiantly thrust out, moist pink lower lip—all combined to make her loving father feel like the lowest of the low for forcing this beautiful creature into scratching and spitting like a frantic, hopelessly trapped kitten.

Lady Penelope could feel the victory that was almost in her grasp; she could sense the weakening in her father's resolve to make her grow up and leave her beloved Weybridge Manor to become some silly man's chattel.

All she had to do now was produce half a dozen convincing tears and perhaps a few heartrending, hiccuping sobs (as she fully recognized that the gravity of her transgression called for extraordinary measures), and the deed would be done. Her father would drop his demand—until the next time—and she would be free to live her life the way she always had, unfettered by convention and answerable to none but her own conscience.

But this time her father was to outmaneuver her. "Very well, child," he relented, "you shall not have to endure this Season you so obviously dread. But it is time you were married. There are three extremely eligible bachelors residing in the neighborhood, all of whom—besotted fools that they are—have applied to me for your hand. Choose a husband from one of them, and I'll have you settled before the new year. That should satisfy your dear departed mother, who is probably watching us from Above right now, poor woman, wringing her hands in distress."

Lady Penelope pressed her palms to her cheeks and shook her head emphatically in the negative. "No, no, no, *no!* Papa, you have missed the point entirely. It is not just the Season that I wish to avoid; it is the subject of marriage in its entirety! What is it, Papa? Do I eat too much? Do I empty your pockets with my demands for gowns and jewelry? Why are you in such a pelter to be shed of me?"

Philo had crossed swords enough times with his intelligent daughter to realize she was trying to trap him with her own twisted brand of logic. If he answered her questions, it would be but the first step down a long tortuous path of questions and arguments that would seem to relate to the subject but, in reality, would only lead to yet another dead end in the convoluted maze that she had constructed in order to put him off.

"Oh no, you don't, missy," he warned, wagging a finger at her. "As I said before—not this time. This time there will be no questions, no debate, no open forum wherein you may express your ridiculous theories about marriage. You are a female of marriageable age, and *you will marry.* That is the beginning, the middle, and the end of it!"

"So much for his oft-expressed love of the Grecian theory of democracy," Lady Penelope muttered under her breath.

"The great dignity and influence enjoyed by wives in ancient Greece is legendary," her father, overhearing, responded. "Wives were revered and loved. You have only to look to your namesake, Penelope, the great love of Odysseus. He endured twenty years of hardship to return to her, while she fended off all suitors for her hand in order to remain true to him."

"Yes, she did, didn't she," Lady Penelope mused quietly, gnawing on her bottom lip. "Quite inventive the dear lady was, too, as I recall. Perhaps I should take a leaf from her book and start weaving. A shroud, wasn't it? I would agree to choose a husband once the shroud was completed, and then unravel each night the work I did during the day. I doubt *my* maid would betray me by informing you of my deception, as poor Penelope's did. What say you, Papa? Would you be agreeable to such a scheme? It is, after all, so very fair—so very *Hellenic.*"

Even as she finished speaking, Lady Penelope knew she had made a fatal mistake. It was not wise to mock the Marquess's deep admiration for things Greek, and it was the absolute height of folly to poke fun at one of their ancient myths. Oh, drat it all, she thought, whenever am I going to learn to curb my heedless tongue! "Papa," she said aloud, holding one hand out to him beseechingly, "I apologize. I can't imagine what made me say such a thing. I—"

"Stubble it, Penny," Philo ordered absently, his bushy black brows furrowing as he concentrated on nurturing the small seed of inspiration that was struggling to burst into bloom. For all his blustering, he hadn't held out much hope for the success of his plans for his daughter's debut into Society—and even less for her agreement to settle upon any of the woeful local specimens of manhood who, if the truth be told, were not exactly what he would have chosen as candidates for a husband to his only daughter.

But now Lady Penelope herself may have unwittingly stumbled on the perfect solution. If he were to challenge her—set her a goal—and outline the penalties if she should fail to perform as agreed, he might just be able to at last manage this unmanageable child. As he paced back and forth between the busts of Socrates and Plato, his keen blue eyes studying their pudgy, bearded faces for inspiration, a slow smile began teasing the corners of his mouth and he breathed softly, "Yes . . . yes, why not?"

"You're smiling, Papa," Lady Penelope pointed out worriedly. "I think I know what you're about—and I'm sure I don't think I like it." She stepped back a few paces, shooting a few quick, longing looks at the gardens just outside the door, while weighing the odds of escaping before her father could issue some sort of ridiculous edict based on an obscure point some long-dead philosopher had scribbled down more than a thousand years before anyone had ever heard of such an inane thing as a London Season.

It was not like her to feel so threatened, but she had tried all her usual ploys with no effect, and something— some strange gleam in her father's eyes—told her that this time she was going to be made to pay the piper.

"That's the ticket! I have it now!" Philo suddenly exclaimed, grabbing the bust of Socrates between his beefy hands and leaning forward to plant a smacking kiss on the cold marble forehead. "And it's fair, too—giving you a sporting chance, Penny, to have your own way after all."

"A wager, Papa?" Lady Penelope asked warily. "Is that what you have in mind?"

"If you care to call it that, yes, a wager. After all, as Herodotus said, 'Force has no place where there is need of skill.' That is what has been wrong all along—I have been trying to employ the use of force; it is skill that is needed when dealing with you."

"Ah," Lady Penelope breathed, relaxing a bit, "you intend to make me a wager and then use your superior skill to maneuver me into losing." She blinded him with one of her dazzling smiles. "How devious of you, dearest. I congratulate you. Tell me, what is this wager?"

Rubbing his hands together in anticipation of his victory, Philo walked across the carpet to stand directly in front of his daughter. "You are to travel to Derbyshire— with your maid, that Dora person, of course—to spend the winter season with your mother's distant cousin, Lucinda Benedict."

"Derbyshire? Good heavens, Papa, why don't you just ship me off to the far side of the moon and have done with it? And her name is Doreen, not Dora. She's Irish, not Greek, no matter what you call her," she countered sarcastically.

"If you'd rather remain here and wed young Lord Perry?" the Marquess suggested, inclining his head indulgently. "As I recall, you've never said you mind his spots."

Lady Penelope wrinkled her small nose in distaste. "I'm sure Derbyshire is absolutely delightful in the wintertime, with all those bare trees and barren hills. Proceed, Papa, I'm listening. I believe you were about to explain this wager of yours."

Her father's smile was almost evil. "Ah, yes, the wager. Very well, child. If you can last out that time without causing a single incident of the sort you have perpetrated today, without engineering a single scandal that has you sent home to me with a nasty note pinned to your cloak, I will never again bring up the subject of a London Season or fight your refusal to look about for a suitable husband."

"And if I fail to behave myself?" Lady Penelope asked, not much liking the smile on her father's face.

"I'm surprised at you, child," Philo teased, feeling a bit full of himself. "It's not like you to even entertain the possibility of failure."

Lady Penelope shrugged her slim shoulders philosophically. "You wouldn't be saying that, dearest Papa, if you could see your face at this moment."

"How fainthearted of you. Very well, I shall not keep you in suspense. If you fail—why, then you shall please me by becoming the most docile, tractable, unexceptionable debutante London has ever seen, comporting yourself with grace and dignity while discreetly casting out lures to prospective suitors for your hand."

"How *utterly* boring."

"The word is 'restful,' my child." The Marquess threaded his fingers together and pushed his hands straight out in front of him, deftly cracking all his knuckles in a gesture of satisfaction that set his daughter's teeth on edge.

She walked over to the pink-veined marble bust of the hapless poet Theognis and placed a hand on the cool stone. Unbidden, a line of his poetry ran through her head:

"Adopt the character of the twisting octopus, which takes on the appearance of the nearby rock. Now follow in this direction, now turn a different hue."

I can do it, she thought, lifting her chin a fraction. After all, what is one dull winter in Derbyshire compared to a lifetime of freedom in my beloved Weybridge?

"Well, daughter?" Philo prodded, still mentally congratulating himself for his genius in having stumbled upon so brilliant a plan. "Don't tell me you're going to cry craven now, just when victory is within your grasp."

Turning to look closely at her father, whose sudden joviality was really quite unnerving, Lady Penelope asked blandly, "Who is this Lucinda Benedict, dear Papa? I don't believe I recall your having spoken of her before. I cannot but wonder—have you somehow stacked the odds in your own favor? Is she some impossible old biddy who will have me slipping vinegar into her morning tea within a fortnight?"

Philo raised a hand to his mouth and covered his smile with a discreet cough. "Lucinda is a distant relative who married a second son and moved to the north of England years ago. Her husband turned up his toes a while back, and one of her husband's relatives—the Dowager Duchess of Avonall—took her in for some time last year in London. I recently heard that the Dowager has been kind enough to set her up on one of the Avonall estates, since the Duke has now married and the chit Lucinda was chaperoning has been popped off as well."

"Why would the Dowager do that?" Lady Penelope asked, tilting her head to one side. "Was she trying to get rid of her, do you think?"

"On the contrary, she was rewarding the old dear for her assistance, I imagine, as I've heard it said young Emily Benedict was a rare handful. She's no great intellect, Lucinda isn't, but if she could manage to bear lead the Duke's flighty sister, she should be able to handle you with no problem. Nor, Penny, is Lucinda some female dragon who will force you into breaking our bargain. That wouldn't be cricket. How could you believe I would do my own daughter such a rum turn?"

Lady Penelope raised her gaze to the stuccoed ceiling

and considered her options. "All right," she said after a time, "I'll accept the wager. But I shall be home the very first warm day of spring to hold you to your end of the bargain. Just think of it!" she exclaimed, holding out her skirts and twirling about in slow circles. "Never again will I have to listen to your little homilies on marriage or endure the mawkish attentions of the suitors you have been pushing at me ever since I passed my seventeenth birthday. Oh, it shall be worth every dreary day I spend in Derbyshire to know that I shall soon be free to be my own person and live my life the way I want!"

Her little explosion of ecstasy over and her usual sunny spirits restored, she kissed her father enthusiastically on both cheeks and scampered off into the gardens to search out her brothers in order to tell them her great news.

Her father stayed behind in the Athenian Room, a strangely devious smile playing about his lips as he mentally prepared his letter to Lucinda Benedict—the most witless, maddeningly eccentric, exasperating widget the good Lord's sense of humor had ever caused Him to create—and a second missive to Hawkins, his majordomo in Grosvenor Square, instructing him to prepare Weybridge Mansion for the Season.

After all, the Marquess of Weybridge solaced himself, for in truth, his fatherly conscience was not quite clear—I never said I would always play fair.

Chapter Three

"THERE is no such thing as a happily married man. The animal simply does not exist."

Philip Rayburn, Earl of Hawkedon, drained his wineglass and looked up owlishly at the man who had just issued this dire condemnation. "Oh, I say, that's rather sweeping, ain't it, Lucien?" he asked his friend, who was just then striking a belligerent pose in front of the massive fireplace. "Surely there must be at least one? Look to your own parents, for example. They've been together well over forty years, and your father seems jolly enough."

"Yes, he does, doesn't he?" Lucien Kenrick, Seventeenth Earl of Leighton, responded, leaning forward slightly to make a wry face at himself as he was reflected in the mirror that hung above the mantelpiece. "That only goes to show you what unlimited blunt and a long string of willing mistresses will do for a man. That, and the fact that dearest Father hasn't drawn a sober breath since his wedding night."

Hawkedon smiled obligingly at this sally.

"No, Philip," Leighton went on with the fervent sagaciousness of the deeply inebriated, "I have studied this subject long and hard, and from every conceivable angle. Marriage, as an institution, was invented by women to serve women. A lucky man may get himself a son to be proud of out of it, but that's all. If it wasn't for succession and entailed estates, I daresay the whole business would completely die out from lack of need. After all, if it's a little frolicking a man wants, there's more than enough willing females to be found—and without having to marry for the privilege."

"Ha! With ideas like yours, Lucien, you should meet

24

my sister, Penelope," Philip quipped before realizing just what he had said.

"Your sister, my friend? My, my, it has been a long time since I've seen you. So you're into pandering now?"

Hawkedon thought furiously for a moment, then colored hotly. *"No!* Wait! That wasn't what I meant at all. Let me rephrase that!"

Leighton suppressed a chuckle. "I should certainly hope so. Please, continue. You have succeeded in capturing my interest. Why should I meet your sister—Penelope, I believe you said her name was? What a delightful appelation."

"I-it's just that Penelope refuses to marry. As a matter of fact, I've had a letter from my brother Cosmo telling me that Papa has just shipped her off to some harebrained cousin of ours named Lucinda Benedict living near Buxton to do penance for refusing to have a Season—m'sister's doing the penance, that is. If she isn't good while she's there, she'll have to have a Season, or some such rot." Shaking his head slightly to clear it, Philip decided too late that he had made a mistake. If there were ever two people in this entire world who should never be allowed to meet, they were Lucien and Penelope. The havoc those two could cause—why, it fairly boggled the mind!

"She would appear to be an intelligent puss," Kenrick commented consideringly. "Near Buxton, you say. Perhaps I should make a stop there on my way north next week; you know, introduce myself as a friend of the family. What does she look like?"

"Penelope?" Philip squeaked, beginning to feel frantic. "Well," he said slowly, as if refreshing his mental picture of his sister. "She's short. Yes, that's it—short. With funny colored hair. And then there's her nose . . . " He trailed off, wrinkling his own nose.

"She has one then? How gratifying. Truly, friend, she sounds delightful," Lucien remarked sarcastically, taking another swallow of his drink.

"Oh, she is, she is!" Philip said bracingly, hoping he sounded as if he were lying through his teeth. "Perhaps you should make it a point to visit her. After all, if anyone could convince her a London Season might be fun, it

25

would be you, as you've certainly enjoyed your share of them.''

''And why should I do that?'' Lucien questioned, eyeing his friend closely. ''Surely you cannot think that the two of us would suit?'' As Philip's neck flushed red, Lucien went on, ''Oh, my dear fellow, you are so transparent! I am the last person you ought to try to play Cupid with, you know.''

''You were always too quick for me, Lucien,'' Philip admitted, averting his eyes. ''Lord, I'm tired,'' he added, slowly nodding while wishing his dratted eyelids wouldn't keep drooping in the middle of this potentially dangerous philosophical discussion. That last verbal encounter had almost landed him in a rare bumblebath! The mantel clock had chimed not so long ago, telling him it was at least two hours past midnight. He and Leighton had been away from their beds since before the break of dawn, traipsing through endless miles of the most uninspiring countryside imaginable, with nothing more to show for their troubles than a pitifully meager game bag, several deep scratches received while freeing one of the hounds from a bramble bush, and two pairs of thoroughly ruined hunting boots.

It was the sudden remembrance of the boots that pushed Philip into saying now: ''Hunting party, ha! I'm willing to believe a body could flush out more game in Piccadilly. And more sport, too, come to think of it.''

''At least Crompton keeps a tolerable cellar,'' Lucien said of their absent host (whose wife had ordered him to bed hours earlier, as if to prove Leighton's point about marriage). Moving away from the fireplace to refill his glass, he concentrated intently on holding the goblet steady while pouring from the heavy cut-crystal decanter. As a few drops of the dark red liquid escaped to run down onto his fine, Dresden lace shirt cuff, he swore softly and backed up a pace. ''Good Lord! I think I'm bosky.''

Squinting in the vain hope the action would improve his blurred vision, Hawkedon assessed the man standing in front of him. Tall, darkly handsome, and impeccably dressed in the subdued style of the departed Brummell, Lucien Kenrick looked as usual to his friend, whose inspection was not so intense as to notice the slight scarlet stain on the Earl's cuff.

"Nonsense, Lucien," Philip contradicted, thankful for the chance to set the conversation off in another direction. "You ain't even slightly foxed. Come to think of it, I've never seen you even a trifle disguised, no matter how many bottles we've broken of an evening. Maybe it's true, what they say—that you're not really human, but some spawn of the netherworld."

Returning to his spot before the mantel, Lucien smiled at his friend, taking in the other man's drink-flushed, youthful blonde features that were the bane of the fellow's existence—for, as Philip had remarked more than once, who took one seriously when one looked like one of Botticelli's damned cherubs?

"Oh, I'm human enough, my friend. Just apply to my mother if you don't believe me. She's told me the tale of how she suffered over my birth *ad nauseam*. Father thanks me for it every time he sees me, since she banished him from her bed from that day forward. But as to never having seen me intoxicated, I do believe I can explain that for you. Without becoming technical, for I fear such a feat to be beyond me at this moment, I should say it has something to do with the fact that you, old son, have absolutely no head for spirits. Why, if I had a pennypiece for every time I have been forced to carry you to your chamber—"

"Oh, ho, Lucien, that reminds me of Billingsley!" Rayburn broke in, partly to change the subject yet again—for his inability to hold his drink was well on its way to becoming legendary—as well as to reminisce about one of Leighton's famous pranks. "Poor George was never the same after that night you and St. John drank him under the table and then slipped him into bed beside the innkeeper's toothless grandmother. Lord, those were the days!"

Philip wrinkled his brow as he pondered a question. "I haven't seen St. John since—come to think of it, I can't at this moment recall the last time I saw him. What a boon companion our friend the Earl of Royston was. Where do you suppose he's gone to anyway?"

"Marriage," Lucien said succinctly, as if that single word proved his earlier point. "The poor fool has gone to marriage. Oh, he vowed to me that he was doing it merely to get himself an heir, but then he retired to his country estate within the year, saying he wanted to be alone with his wife, and nobody's seen hide nor hair of him since. He was one of the first to go. Surely you can't have forgotten it.''

"I remember his wife—Samantha, wasn't it?'' Hawkedon put in quietly, resigned to the fact that Leighton wasn't to be diverted, no matter how he tried. Who would have thought talking about Zachary St. John would lead them right back to the subject of marriage? Why, oh why, he groaned inwardly, did his friend have to climb upon this particular hobbyhorse tonight? Next thing Philip knew, Lucien would be waxing lyrical about that crazy vow they all took years ago, one fateful night at White's when they were all deep in their cups. "Pretty little thing,'' he added, conjuring up a mental picture of the Earl of Royston's bride.

"They're the worst kind. One minute you think you're in charge, and the next minute some pretty piece of fluff has you so tied up in knots you can't take a deep breath without her permission. I hear Zachary already has one son, and yet another brat on the way. He must be miserable.''

Philip considered this for a moment. "He might be,'' he said at last, grinning, "but chances are the fellow ain't figured it out yet.''

Lucien raised his quizzing glass to his eye and studied his friend, who was at that moment smiling vacantly into his glass. "First this business about introducing me to your sister and her 'nose,' and now this defense of Royston's wife. You know, you're beginning to worry me, Philip,'' he said solemnly. "I know we haven't really been in touch for nearly a year, what with my having to take over the reins on m'father's estates while he was laid up with the gout, but could it be you've forgotten our vow? That's why I was so happy that fool Crompton allowed me to join you here when I was at last able to break free—so that we could spend some time together. But you seem preoccupied, and have all week. Tell me, has some dewy-eyed debutante muddled your mind or has your father cut off your allowance?''

Hawkedon shook his head in violent denial, nearly unsettling the contents of his stomach. ''Philo wouldn't do that to his oldest son, the light of his eye. No, I'm very well to fly, thank you—and I'm *not* about to throw myself away on some milk and water puss. What odd ideas you get into your head; I scarcely can believe it! Besides, a vow is a vow, even if we all were bloody lushy when we decided on it. I am not disposed to breaking the thing by willingly putting my neck in the parson's mousetrap. How could you believe your best friend capable of deceit? Single we swore to be and single *I*, for one, shall remain! Long live bachelorhood! *Ow!* I should stay away from dramatics. That hurt my head. Lucien, what say we call it a day? After all, the hunt continues in the morning.''

''May as well be hunting mare's nests, for all the luck we'll have,'' Leighton observed, only slightly mollified by his friend's impassioned defense of his motives. ''I tell you, Philip, if Crompton cannot come up with some better sport soon, I shall be forced into taking myself off before the week is out and heading on up to Scotland earlier than I had planned. I feel the need of some excitement, and Lord knows London is flat this time of year. We could even stop in at this Benedict woman's household and visit your sister—the one with the nose. You with me?''

Now Philip was in a quandary. While he agreed with Lucien that Crompton's idea of a house party put him more in mind of a long Sunday afternoon spent in the Vicar's fusty parlor, Philip knew that Lady Redfern and her daughter Dorinda were due to arrive at the estate over the weekend. Why else had he accepted Crompton's invitation in the first place? he reminded himself ruefully. Pretty little puss, Dorinda was, though Philip would die before he'd tell Lucien that he'd fairly well decided to make a determined push at the girl. After all, there was that damnable vow to consider. Oh, why did his friend have to pop back into the picture now?

''Well?'' Leighton prodded, as his friend rapidly removed the guilt-stricken look from his face. ''Don't tell me you like it here, friend, for it won't wash. Or do you have something against Scotland?''

"Yes! That's it!" Philip exclaimed, thankfully jumping on this explanation. "Horrid, cold, damp spot. Never did like that benighted country above half. Besides, anyone can tell you I can't abide salmon. The damned fish makes me break out in spots, you know. And it's *red* inside." He pulled a face. "Disgusting."

Lucien looked at his companion levelly for several long, uncomfortable moments. "Redfern. Dorinda Redfern," he pronounced at last, his voice cold.

Philip's wide blue eyes shifted from side to side as he cudgeled his brain for a way out of this tight spot. Lucien was a good friend, but it wasn't wise to get on his wrong side. There was no telling what the man might do to you. "W-Who?" he stammered at last, reaching out to refill his glass. "The name's slightly familiar, but I don't think I can picture the face."

Leighton smiled kindly. "Oh, of course you can, my friend. I heard she's to be Crompton's houseguest this weekend, as a matter of fact. Grotesque bleached creature, as I recall, with bad teeth."

"She is not! She's gorgeous! A veritable angel!" Philip Rayburn exploded before realizing he had been neatly maneuvered into betraying his true reason for turning down his friend's invitation. "You sly dog!" he said admiringly before warily sinking back against the chair cushion, wondering what Lucien would do next.

"Yes, I am, aren't I, for I refuse to be crass and point out the fact that you are such an elementary puzzle to solve," Leighton acknowledged, bowing slightly from the waist. "It's a pity, though, that you could not have been more open with me, Philip, more honest."

"You're not going to call me out or anything, are you, Lucien?" the blonde cherub asked worriedly, wishing very hard that he could close his eyes and wake up in his warm bed, with the remainder of this conversation behind him. "After all, it was a silly vow. Royston wasn't the first of our group to break it, getting bracketed to a young hoyden who went about tossing strawberry tarts in people's faces. Nick Mannering broke it as well—twice, although he only married once, to crazy old Saxon's Yankee granddaughter of all people. And don't forget Tony Betancourt, causing all that to-do by marrying that Murphy girl—some unknown Irish chit. Lord, man, it ain't like I'm doing anything the rest of our group hasn't already done. Right? Besides, I'd be the only one of us to wed a *normal* female, if you ask me. That should mean something."

Lucien folded his hands together in front of him and let out a resigned sigh. "Please don't build up any false hopes waiting for me to present you with a medal for your minor triumph. You and I were the only ones left, Philip, the only ones to remain true to our convictions. Why do you think I was so eager to see you after being stuck in the country so long? Now you, too, are on your way to breaking our vow. You must have hated it when I showed up here this week, seeking out my old friend just when you were about to declare yourself to the Redfern chit."

"No, I—" Philip protested weakly.

"Well, I won't stand here and lie to you, saying that it doesn't matter to me," Lucien pushed on relentlessly, "knowing that your cruel defection will leave me the last sane man in all of England, but I can see now that there is nothing else for it but to wish you happy and then go crawling off to Scotland alone to nurse my wounds, a broken, thoroughly disillusioned man."

Philip was feeling very uncomfortable, and his restless squirming in the huge leather wing chair confirmed it. "Damn it, Leighton, I ain't bracketed yet! And I was very glad to see you—bloody overjoyed, as a matter of fact! Besides, for all I know, she won't have me."

"Oh, she'll have you all right," Lucien prophesied gloomily. "Oldest son of a Marquess? Her Mama would have her head for a pincushion if she dared turn down such a prize. How does that make you feel, Philip—to be considered as a prize, a titled trophy to be hung on Lady Redfern's drawing room wall? What a noble end for a man like you."

The Earl of Hawkedon rose unsteadily to his feet and peered at his friend through the predawn gloom. "You know what it is, Lucien. You're jealous. Yes, you are," he pushed on, pot-valiant, before his friend could interrupt him. "All right, so we went along with you all those years ago when you suggested we take a vow of eternal, heart-free bachelorhood. I'm sure we weren't the only ones to make silly vows during our salad days. But that doesn't mean that we have to abide by such foolishness now, by God! The others have married, and happily, too, from all accounts. You're the only one who refuses to see that we are men now, with all the responsibilities of our station in life."

"Meaning?" Lucien urged, his dark eyes dangerously narrowed.

"Meaning," Philip went on hastily, before his courage could desert him, "that you have refused to grow up and face *your* responsibilities. Meaning that you are still playing pranks and acting the carefree young blade long past the time for putting away childish things. Why, you're the only man I know who actually frolicked your way through the war, organizing mule races between battles and raiding henhouses after Wellington expressly warned us against such things. And that curtsying contest you arranged for all those toothless, flea-ridden señoritas—oh, why should I go on?" Thrusting out his chin defiantly—as he may as well be hung for a sheep as a lamb—he then ended, *"Meaning,* Dorinda Redfern is the most beautiful, adorable creature who ever walked on God's green earth, and I'm going to by-damn wed her whether *you* like it or not!"

"You're drunk," Leighton observed mildly, his eyes suddenly shuttered.

"You're damned right, I am!" the angelic-looking Earl of Hawkedon agreed, reaching out to grab a chair before he fell flat on his face. "Why else do you think I said what I just said? Lord, I must be out of my mind! Please, Lucien, forgive me. It's just that I've been cudgeling my brain all week long to find a way to tell you about Miss Redfern and myself . . . and then you went and brought up that ridiculous vow . . . and then you tricked me into admitting it, and . . . oh, hell, I think I'm going to be sick! Quickly, Lucien, will you forgive me?"

Moving swiftly to open the French doors that led out to the first floor balcony so that his friend could cast up his accounts over the stone railing into the garden, Lucien said most graciously: "Of course I forgive you, Philip. Don't give it another thought."

The Earl of Hawkedon woke slowly late the next morning, the thin, watery sunlight coming in through the small, uncurtained window causing twin lightning bolts to be visible behind his tightly closed eyelids. The second thought to enter his dully throbbing head—the first being a vague question as to how he had gotten to bed in the first place—was to marvel at his temerity in confronting Lucien Kenrick so boldly concerning that man's aversion to marriage.

Had he really said all those things to his friend? Even taken him to task about his love of pranking and irreverent way of looking at life? Eyes still shut against the day, Philip's face took on a rather smug expression as he complimented himself on his daring—even if it had taken a good six bottles of burgundy and a crushing hangover to accomplish the feat.

Lucien had surprised him, Philip realized as he began to shift his body slightly (after taking the time to curse his host for providing such rocklike, lumpy beds for his guests, and his valet for failing to draw the drapery against the sun), handling the criticism like a man and even complimenting Philip on his decision to become "domesticated."

"I should be ashamed of myself for underestimating him," Philip scolded himself sternly as he made to turn on his side, seeking a more comfortable resting place. The bed was so rock hard—and the room smelled musty, too! Damn Crompton for a pinch-penny bastard! "I thought sure Lucien would have my guts for garters," he continued, still keeping his eyes tightly shut as he blindly reached out to locate another pillow for his aching head.

I owe Lucien an apology, sure as check. Perhaps I'll even be able to convince him to stay here until after Dorinda and her mother have gone, and then I'll go with him to Scotland, or wherever else it is he wants to go. At last, opening his eyes reluctantly, he groused ill-naturedly, "Now where in blazes is that pil—*Good God, who's that?*"

Visions of the innkeeper's toothless grandmother filling

33

him with trepidation, Philip quickly pulled back his hand as if he had been burnt, then cast his gaze about Crompton's crowded larder, where he had somehow come to spend the night lying across half a dozen sacks of flour.

"I'll kill Leighton for this!" the Earl vowed earnestly before prudently scampering over to the nearby wall on his hindquarters and gingerly pulling away the thin blanket that had served both he and whatever it was that was sharing his lumpy bed.

His nose told him moments before his eyes confirmed it. He had spent the night tucked up beside the cold, scaly, vacant-eyed body of a truly gigantic salmon—a salmon incongruously dressed in a white lawn nightgown and makeshift wedding veil.

"Damn the man!"

Lucien Kenrick had struck again.

Chapter Four

"You do realize, of course, Doreen, that this means war!"

Doreen Fiona Elizabeth Sweeney, Lady Penelope Rayburn's personal maid and confidante, stopped in the midst of hanging one of her mistress's gowns in the great, ugly carved-wood cabinet and perked up her ears. She had thought something was rather havey-cavey about this out of the way place from the moment the two of them had set foot in it just after the noon hour that day and seen Farnley, the strange, gloomy-eyed butler. Now her suspicions seemed to have been confirmed. "And why would that be, milady, I'm askin', seein' as how you've only just met your keeper? What's the trouble—is she some fire and brimstone merchant?"

Lady Penelope boosted her small frame onto the high platform bed, leaving her feet dangling some ten inches above the floor. "No, Doreen, Aunt Lucinda is no monster," she said ruefully. "Would that she were. I'd know how to handle that. But it's not that simple. What Aunt Lucinda is—is a Bedlamite. And even worse, she's a *likeable* Bedlamite!"

Doreen looked at her mistress inquiringly. "A few slates off the old girl's roof, you'd say?"

Lady Penelope snorted in a most unladylike way. "Half the structure is gone, I'd say. Wait 'till you see her, Doreen. The woman's an absolute original! She must be sixty if she's a day, and she dresses like a debutante in her first Season—all frills and bows and foaming draperies. But that's not the worst of it. Oh no, it is much more than that."

"Well, I should certainly hope so," Doreen countered

matter-of-factly. She resumed her unpacking, for she was the sort who would rather have unpleasant chores out of the way. "It would take more than a vain old lady with a likin' for shingerleens to set *me* off, don't you know."

Tossing her head saucily at this mild rebuke, Lady Penelope hopped lightly down from the bed and flounced over to stand in front of her maid, looking up at the much taller, broader, older woman. "All right, Doreen," she challenged hotly, "let's see what you think of this! Aunt Lucinda doesn't use normal conversation to talk to a person. The dratted woman speaks only in *quotes!*"

"And now it's funnin' me you are, aren't you?" Doreen asked softly, looking askance at her mistress, whose full, pink bottom lip was thrust out defiantly.

"Really?" Lady Penelope taunted, feeling rather gratified at being able to startle her maid. "Then answer me this, Doreen. Why, when I was ushered into her presence, did Aunt Lucinda return my greeting by saying, 'For I, who hold sage Homer's rule the best, welcome the coming, speed the going guest,' and then mutter the name 'Pope'?"

"Homer?" Doreen repeated, pondering the quote. "That would be one of the Marquess's Greek cronies, wouldn't it, milady? Perhaps the old dear was trying to make you feel to home—seein' as how your da is always spoutin' some such drivel. Look how he calls me Dora. Not that I mind, you know, as long as nobody calls me late to supper."

Lady Penelope shook her head in disgusted dismissal of such an explanation. "I thought that at first myself, Doreen," she said, turning to examine her reflection in the large, cloudy pier glass that hung above an ornate Chinese table in the large bedchamber. "Lord, but this house is crammed full of some of the ugliest furniture I have ever seen! But never mind that now. After I had introduced myself to my aunt and thanked her for being so kind as to open her house to me after my father fairly *banished* me from my own home, she only hugged me tightly against her and said in this so-sad voice, 'What's mine is yours.' Oh yes, that was from the bard's *Measure for Measure,* I think. Can you fathom it, Doreen? I believe the ridiculous widget thinks I am some poor, misused waif, and she's going to shelter me from the storm—meaning Papa, of course.''

"What a dear, darlin' lady,'' Doreen remarked, longing to catch a glimpse of Lucinda Benedict.

"Of course she is! But however can I help but play pranks on such a sweet, *simple* soul, much as I should be ashamed of myself for doing so? Why, it would be like being shown a room filled waist deep with delicious Gunther ices and then being locked in there without a spoon. I would go out of my mind! Oh, Papa is so deep, so very clever! He knew what he was about, all right, when he did this to me. He'll have me bracketed to some simpering London dandy before I can so much as mount a token resistance! And he said he was being aboveboard with me. I should have known better than to trust him when he's got his own best interests at heart. Men are abominable—all of them!''

Doreen threw back her head and laughed in real enjoyment. "Oh, milady, 'tis grand to listen to you in a rage, and that's a fact. And your da—why, the old devil must be chucklin' up his sleeve a real treat right now. Here now, stop that, do!''

The maid quickly slapped down Lady Penelope's hands before the younger woman's harsh treatment of her buttons could totally destroy the kelly green traveling gown.

"You're a cheeky Irishwoman, Doreen, I'll give you that,'' Lady Penelope jibed halfheartedly, trying hard to stand still while the maid unhooked the dozens of small, covered buttons that held her trapped within the gown. "Hurry, please, and then search out my riding habit. Nemesis should be rested enough to bear with me while I have a bit of a run. I need to clear the cobwebs out of my head—think about this horrible thing Papa has done to me—before I decide on a plan of action.''

"When needs must, the devil drives,'' Doreen muttered under her breath, seeing the shining green eyes and flushed cheeks of her mistress reflected in the pier glass. "And it's careful you'll be, milady, else they'll be bringin' you home on a fence gate and no mistake. That horse is a terror. Here now, stand still whilst I put this over your head.''

Five frantic minutes later, her long mane of red-gold hair tied back haphazardly at her nape, and the jaunty shako hat that matched her deep blue velvet riding habit slammed down low over her forehead, Lady Penelope Rayburn descended the stairs to the foyer of the country house, her riding crop rhythmically slap-slapping against her thigh as she beat out a silent, condemning litany concerning scheming fathers, eccentric aunts, and Society in general.

Lucinda Benedict, who had just finished the single glass of sherry she allowed herself each afternoon, entered the foyer from the small drawing room just as her houseguest reached the front door ahead of a scurrying footman. Smiling benignly, Lucinda spread her arms wide and quoted: '' 'Bright youth passes swiftly as a thought,' Theognis.''

Hesitating for but a moment, a shiver of irritation skittering lightly down her back, Lady Penelope Rayburn gave in to impulse and countered, '' 'You may as well go to hell with a load as with a bundle!' Doreen Fiona Elizabeth Sweeney.''

Once the door had slammed behind her guest's rapidly departing back, Lucinda, her brow furrowed in thought, moved her painted lips silently as she committed the quote to memory, wondering just who this Sweeney person was and why she had never read any of her work.

Having departed Lord Crompton's rambling estate just south of Ashbourne on horseback at a little past noon, the Earl of Leighton had entered almost immediately into that area of Derbyshire called "The Peak"—a rather hilly stretch of countryside which, however inspiring it might be to its residents or summer visitors, left a lot to be desired in the way of scenery on this damp, dreary late-November day.

His horse being quite fresh, and with a substantial supply of food in his pack—the latter having been delivered personally into the Earl's hands by the Crompton chef, whose pockets had become much plumper due to his willingness to turn his back while one of his best salmon went missing—Lucien Kenrick decided to try his luck on one of the country lanes that branched off the main roadway just outside Buxton, hoping to circumvent the town and its traffic.

He'd set no real pattern for his travels, after all, except to plan upon meeting up with his traveling coach and valet in Edinburgh at the end of the week, believing this to be a perfect opportunity to get to know the vagaries of the huge stallion he'd had the luck to acquire just that week at a local horse fair—a coal-black, moody brute his friend Hawkedon had christened "Hades."

"Perhaps I am being overly nice about this, but considering the trick I played on poor Philip back there at Crompton's," he murmured aloud as he rode along, "I do believe I shall be so kind as to give the 'Nose' a miss this time around. After all, the poor boy will have suffering enough to deal with once Lady Redfern sinks her hooks into him."

What he didn't dwell on, what he refused to dwell on, was his unease at having put Hawkedon through the hoops so badly, when in truth it was Lucien's own past sins that had prompted him that long-ago evening to propose the asinine vow to never marry, his own brief personal experience with the institution of marriage having soured him, his own pain and disillusionment having prejudiced him.

"But Philip doesn't know—and shall *never* know," Lucien promised himself aloud. "Besides, that's all ancient history now. I can't imagine why I should be thinking of it at all. Perhaps I should have given Scotland a miss as well. Ah, alas, Hades, it's too late now, isn't it, with my coach already on its way to Edinburgh?"

He hadn't gone more than a few miles on the country road before he realized that he was traveling east rather than north, and he was ready to turn his mount about when he thought he caught a quick flash of color out of the corner of his eye. Turning slightly in his saddle, Leighton could make out the figures of a single horse and rider galloping along the bare field behind the thin row of trees alongside the lane.

The horse, a great, hulking gray gelding with long, pale-as-smoke mane and tail, appeared almost to be flying across the uneven ground, his flashing hooves throwing up huge clumps of wet earth, his nostrils breathing hot puffs of steam into the cold air.

But it wasn't the horse—magnificent beast that it was—that caught the Earl's attention, but rather the diminutive female rider atop the sidesaddle strapped to it that captured and held his interested gaze. She was dressed head to toe in lush midnight-blue velvet, her full skirts billowing out to cover the gelding's rump while her unbound hair whipped about in the wind like long fingers of liquid flame.

"I'll soon be waxing poetic, by God," Lucien marveled aloud before deciding that, although he could be excused for thinking that he was witnessing a damsel in distress being carried off by a runaway horse, what he was actually seeing was a masterful horsewoman in the midst of putting her equally impressive mount through its paces. She must have outrun her groom from the moment she left the stables.

"So why am I sitting here like some brainless bumpkin with his fingers stuck in his mouth, eh, Hades?" he asked his stallion, who had been prancing and sidestepping impatiently for some moments, eager for a run that would prove to that showy gray plug just who was the better horse. "Right you are then, my boy," Leighton said, pushing his heels lightly into the stallion's quivering flanks. "We could both do with a bit of a romp. Let's have at it!"

Then they were off like the proverbial shot, racing along the gravel lane running parallel to the path taken by the gelding, crossing over into the field just as soon as a small break in the trees allowed, and within less than a minute Hades had pulled to within three lengths of the other horse.

The sound of Hades's pounding hooves coming up close behind her caught Lady Penelope's attention, and she turned her head, looking back over her shoulder through a tangled curtain of hair. Emerald eyes flashing fire, she quickly took the measure of both the horse and its elegantly dressed rider in one assessing glance, and her small pointed chin lifted a fraction as she silently acknowledged the challenge she and her mount had been issued.

Leighton couldn't know it, but he was offering Lady

Penelope just the diversion she craved—a mind-clearing race, not to mention a chance to get a little of her own back against one of those most infuriating creatures: a Man. The gelding lengthened its distance-eating strides even as she blighted her pursuer with a dazzling smile, and in a moment the gap between the two horses had increased from three lengths to five.

The pure, flawless beauty of the face Lady Penelope had presented to him had nearly caused Lucien to be unhorsed, but the infuriatingly smug smile that had flashed across those same perfect features put new resolve into what had begun as a purely sporting adventure. Typical female, he thought idly, refusing to believe that a woman—regardless of the caliber of her mount—could best a man in any sport. "Very well, madam," he breathed softly, "never let it be said that I disappointed a lady. If it's a race you want, then it's a race you shall get."

Leaning his head low against his horse's neck, his elbows close to his sides as he urged Hades along, Leighton concentrated on closing the gap between the two mounts before they reached the end of the clearing and were forced to stop.

While Lucien remained coolly detached, and even a bit amused, Lady Penelope's heart was racing in time with Nemesis's rapidly pounding hoofbeats. How both she and her mount loved a challenge! She felt the wind tug at her shako hat, sending it winging away into the muddy field. Since the ribbon Doreen had tied in her hair had long ago met a similar fate, Lady Penelope's long, red-gold tresses were now completely free to blow in the wind, trailing along behind her like the fiery, glowing tail of some speeding comet. She took a moment to shake her head about, then lifted her face to the sun and laughed aloud.

"My God, Hades, the little vixen is loving every moment of this!" Lucien exclaimed, suddenly short of breath.

He was right. Another young, unchaperoned female might have been feeling more than a little apprehensive about the sudden appearance of a stranger when she was abroad alone and in unfamiliar countryside—a stranger who for all intents and purposes seemed to be pursuing her—but it must be remembered that Lady Penelope Rayburn had never been accused of being a "usual" sort of female.

Having ridden the lands around Weybridge Manor unfettered since she was old enough to sit a horse (and having grown up amid an atmosphere of constant friendly competition, courtesy of her three hey-go-mad older brothers), she was at the moment merely reacting with her usual exuberance, thrilled to be able to show her darling Nemesis to his best advantage against the massive black stallion—and the rider who was laboring under the misapprehension that there existed a single bit of horseflesh in the entirety of the British Isles capable of overtaking Nemesis in a fair race.

Besides, Lady Penelope thought—for, after all, she was nineteen and not such a blockhead as to think the world was populated with none but gentlemen of sterling good manners who would not dream of taking unfair advantage of a young, unchaperoned woman—it was not as if she were entirely helpless!

Reaching one gloved hand down to lift the thin leather flap located on one side of the sidesaddle her father had presented her with the year before, she slid out the slim, jeweled silver stiletto hidden in the specially sewn pocket and slipped it up her sleeve. "A pretty toy," her brother Philippos had called it, but then Philippos had never seen her throw the weapon against a target (a ludicrous caricature of Napoleon Bonaparte's head atop the body of a frog) with the deadly accuracy acquired through long months of practice behind the stables.

She knew she dared not take the time to look back again at the pursuing horse. No more than a hundred yards of the field remained to be covered before one of the riders could claim victory, and Lady Penelope turned her full attention to the race, leaning low over Nemesis's neck and whispering encouragement into the horse's ear. "Fly, my beautiful darling," she urged passionately, her heart pounding wildly in her throat. "Fly like the very wind!"

The trees seemed to whiz by them on either side as the two riders leant their full concentration to the race; their mounts straining against their leads as the field in front of them rapidly disappeared and the lichen-covered stone wall that marked the end of the open area loomed menacingly in the foreground.

"Stupid chit!" Lucien rasped, a small trickle of fear skipping up his spine as he decided that the girl was going to try to clear the high wall separating the field from the meadow lying on the other side. "This is taking fun too far, Hades!"

His concern for the other rider in the forefront of his mind, the Earl then did something he had never before done to a horse of his—he dug his heels ruthlessly into his mount's sides, desperate to reach the girl and sweep her from the sidesaddle before the gelding could attempt the dangerous jump. It was a mad plan, but the whole race had been badly planned from the start, and it was now up to him to save the day before the headstrong girl broke her lovely but silly neck.

Hades, who had been well named for the Prince of Darkness, responded to his new master's harsh treatment by rolling his huge, red-rimmed eyes wildly, whipping his massive head about, and clamping the dislodged bit down firmly between his teeth. So it was a race his master wanted, was it? Well then, Hades would give the Earl the ride of his life!

Aware that somehow he and Hades had just exchanged roles, Lucien cursed sharply and hauled viciously on the reins, sacrificing good horsemanship for expediency—for now the girl was not the only rider in danger. Hades was heading straight for the stone wall, and there was nothing Lucien could do to stop him.

For one fleeting moment Lucien wished himself and his fragile neck safely and boringly back at Crompton's, sloshing through some bog where he stood a great chance of catching cold and little else. That thought was quickly dashed, however, when he recalled the fact that his continued presence at the house party would necessitate his being a witness to the downfall of Philip Rayburn, his last unattached friend, and he knew he would rather face a hundred stone walls than spend so much as a single evening sitting across the dinner table from Dorinda Redfern's calculating mama.

Chancing another quick look toward the foam-flecked

gelding, and mentally measuring the distance between the two horses and the wall, Lucien gave up any lingering hope that he could gain control of Hades and still have time to pluck the female to safety. He closed his eyes and whispered a silent prayer that the other rider knew the lay of the land well enough to be sure that the other side of the wall provided a clear space for landing and recovery. Then, realizing full well that he really had been given no choice in the matter, he stopped trying to fight Hades and tightened his knees about the animal's muscled sides, readying himself for the jump.

It could only be deemed a pity that the two racers could not have spared a moment or two for conversation, for the passage of only a few words between them would have been enough to clear up Lucien's misconception as to Lady Penelope's knowledge of the countryside—and vice versa.

Leery of putting Nemesis at an unknown obstacle, Lady Penelope originally had planned to pull up short of the wall, a clear winner in the impromptu race. But her opponent had proved worthy, and there was no way she could take the time to slow her mount and still be sure of an undisputed victory. Obviously her opponent was a local gentleman, she assured herself, taking the time for one more look at Leighton over her shoulder. He was showing no sign of reining in his mount. Clearly he intended to jump that showy stallion over the wall to the other side and then claim victory, leaving her on the near side, looking foolish and cowardly.

Well, not if she had anything to say in the matter, he wasn't! she thought mulishly, giving her mount its head. She was still in the lead, and she was going to win! By the time that black monster was halfway over the wall, she, Lady Penelope Rayburn, would be sitting smugly atop her own mount on the other side, inspecting the tip of her right glove while politely waiting to accept the gentleman's congratulations.

The two horses approached the wall, the gelding still a length and a half in front, and Lady Penelope could feel Nemesis's muscles gathering for the jump. With the thundering noise of the horses' hooves echoing in her ears and competing with the loud beating of her own heart, Lady

Penelope eased her slight body forward, making herself as one with the gelding, already anticipating both the thrill of hurling through the air and the jolt of the landing.

Nemesis's front hooves left the ground, the rest of the gelding's body following in a sort of liquid grace, and Lady Penelope only had time to suck in her breath and give one startled look back at the other rider before kicking herself free of the stirrup and throwing her body clear as Nemesis tried vainly to twist in midair, desperate to avoid the empty hay cart that lay propped against the other side of the wall.

She landed rudely, rump first, in the middle of a patch of frost-wilted wildflowers, her breath knocked out of her but otherwise unharmed, and watched wide-eyed as Nemesis did an ungainly half-somersault just beyond the deadly reach of the wooden hay cart. Then, before the gelding could regain its feet, Lady Penelope caught sight of the black stallion, his massive, girded belly not ten feet above her head, following the exact unhappy path she and her mount had traveled only a split second or two earlier.

The sun was momentarily placed in shadow as the beast seemed to hover above her before passing on, to land cleanly on its front legs beside Nemesis. The stallion's rider, however, returned to earth separately, his landing not nearly so well executed, his head making fleeting contact with one of the wooden poles of the hay cart just a moment before his body collapsed in a most awkward crumpled position at Lady Penelope's feet.

Chapter Five

THERE was a loud, irritating buzzing in his ears, an intrusive noise that rose and fell, then rose again, setting off a tremendous thump-thumping deep inside his head that was far worse than any hangover he could remember. No, he thought slowly, I don't think I've been drinking. I've been riding; on my way to Scotland, I believe. He squeezed his eyes tightly shut against the pain of thinking. There had been a horse—and a girl. A lovely, fiery-haired creature. A wild race across country. A high stone wall.

Damn!

He wanted to moan at his returning memory, but realized such self-indulgence would take too much effort. He'd come a cropper, he recalled with some shame, sailing off the saddle in the middle of a jump like some green looby who couldn't be trusted to keep a tolerable seat on a plowhorse.

The last thing he could recall with any measure of clarity was twisting his head about frantically in time to see the beautiful female rider—the one he had been out to impress, the one he was so sure had been about to come to grief—sitting safe and unharmed on a soft carpet of vegetation, taking a front row seat, as it were, while he proceeded to make a bloody idiot of himself.

Once he had mentally filled in the blanks on all the questions buffeting back and forth inside his aching head, Lucien decided that the female must have summoned help, for nothing else could explain the fact that he was sure he was now lying on a comfortable bed rather than the rocky ground. Another man might have immediately felt grateful for the rescue, but Leighton could not help but consider the fact that if it hadn't been for the dratted woman's obvious baiting of him, he probably would never have taken the fall in the first place.

For if his head was hurting, that ache was as nothing when compared to the massive mental pain now raging through his male pride. How his friend Philip would laugh at his predicament, Lucien thought ruefully. The dear boy would be overjoyed to see me put at such a disadvantage; he'd probably tell me it was my own fault and then slip a pair of salmon into bed on either side of me for good measure.

As men are not generally known to dwell on thoughts that tend to show them at a disadvantage, Lucien returned his attention to his immediate physical surroundings. Slowly, painfully, his muddled mind concentrating on the sounds he heard coming from some far corner of the room, he decided that it must have been the muffled noise of voices raised in anger that had so rudely intruded on his peace a few minutes earlier.

He struggled to identify the voices. Female. Two of them, jabbering away nineteen to the dozen. Ignorant chippies! Couldn't they tell he was trying to sleep? How could they be so featherbrained, so typically female? Why didn't they shut up and leave him alone?

"You're being ridiculous, Doreen," Lady Penelope was saying, not even trying to keep her voice low, as the man lying in her bed had been unconscious for over two hours and she saw no need to whisper. "You heard the doctor, idiot bumpkin leech though he was. What you're suggesting is the height of folly. The man simply cannot be moved again. Any more upset, and it could prove fatal."

Fatal? Lucien, overhearing, repeated silently, momentarily startled out of his bad humor. *Good Lord, how badly am I hurt?* He tried again to open his eyes, but even this simple exercise proved costly, and he quickly abandoned the effort as he steeled himself against yet another onslaught of pain. Hey there, you tabbies, he called out mentally, you've got a man dying over here. Do you think you could cease and desist your pointless wrangling for a moment to come over here and hold my hand as I utter my last words?

"Then mayhap can you be tellin' me where it is that you're supposed to sleep, milady, what with that great hulkin' carcass layin' smack in the middle of your bed?" the second voice—obviously that of a servant, and painfully shrill to the Earl's way of thinking—asked belligerently.

What are you worrying about, you daft woman? he groused silently. If I'm dying, your mistress will have her dratted bed back soon enough. There was just no pleasing a woman, he rued with a small smirk, boosting his flagging spirits a trifle. Well, Lucien decided, about to stick his spoon in the wall or nay, he'd by God had more than enough of this caterwauling. "Why don't you two chattering magpies put a muzzle on it and flutter off to leave me die in peace?" he growled irritably.

"How dare you, sirrah!" Lady Penelope declared at once, her husky voice openly challenging as she whirled in the direction of the huge bed. "You will kindly stay out of this conversation. *Oh, my goodness, Doreen!* How stupid of me! He's awake! Quickly, see if you can catch up with that silly doctor before he scampers off."

"Yes, Doreen, dearest, why don't you do that?" Lucien agreed nastily from his rack of pain. "Perhaps then he will be so kind as to provide you with a nice thick bandage with which you can stuff up your mistress's mouth."

The maid quickly looked back and forth between her glowering mistress and their rude patient, sniffing the tension that suddenly hung thick in the air between the two. "You know I can't leave you alone with him, milady," she pointed out in a fierce whisper, firmly placing her hands on her ample hips. "It wouldn't be fittin', and that's a fact. Besides, if he keeps up with openin' his potato trap like that, you might just take it into your head to murder him before I get back. I can see that look in your eyes."

Lady Penelope took hold of the servant's upper arm and steered her toward the open doorway. "Don't be silly. This is no time to be worrying about propriety. Besides, he's probably just delirious," she added under her breath, just as if she had not, in fact, been entertaining the pleasure she would doubtless derive from throttling the ungrateful brute. "The man has a wrenched ankle, three cracked ribs, and a bump on his head the size of a turnip. I scarcely think he's in any condition to toss me onto the carpet and ravish me. Now, go!" She then shoved Doreen inelegantly out of the room, loudly slamming the door on the flustered maid's departing back.

From behind her, Lady Penelope could hear every low, forceful word of the pithy epithet Lucien Kenrick was using to colorfully describe any female so sapskulled as to shoot off a brace of cannon while a man was trying to concentrate on producing an articulate death rattle.

Turning around just in time to see her patient employing one shaky hand to inspect the heavy white bindings that half-covered his head, Lady Penelope warned loudly, "Stop touching that bandage. Keep your hand down! You have to remain still, you fool. You've had an accident, and you're badly hurt. Though I must say I'm beginning to feel that it's more than just a slight shame that you didn't manage to break your jawbone while you were about it, for it would have made my job that much easier."

"I love you, too, sweetings," Leighton responded tightly, trying once more to open his eyes. He did, however, return his hand to his side, not because of Lady Penelope's order, but because just that small bit of movement had left him feeling as if he had broken every second bone in his pain-racked body. He amended his plans for a self-examination, thinking it best to wait upon the doctor's return before he inadvertently did himself any more damage.

What he would concentrate on now was the mighty effort of opening his eyes. Realizing that the pressure on his forehead came from the heavy bandage that was pressing down hard on his eyebrows, he stopped fighting it and merely raised his eyelids a fraction, looking down toward the end of the bed and the slim female body that stood there, arms crossed at the waist.

His vision was limited to the central area of her body, but it was sufficient to tell him that he was looking at his recent racing companion. "Blue, one of my favorite colors," he remarked, recalling the riding habit he had chased the length of some farmer's field. "What are you doing here anyway? Shouldn't you be off somewhere, embroidering slippers or something? Ladies are of no use in a sickroom.''

Out of a long list of comments Lucien could have made, he had unerringly lighted on the one thing that was sure to set Lady Penelope soaring off into the treetops with anger. After all, she had just spent a very trying few hours. All that had been required of him was that he lie quietly, while it was left to her to do all the work!

She had been ignominiously tossed off her horse and flung onto the hard ground, somehow inflicting a fatal tear to the skirt of her absolutely favorite riding habit. She had then been scared witless, believing that the man now lying in her bed making cutting remarks at her expense had been killed because of her juvenile wish for a bit of frolic.

The entire time she had been rounding up the two horses—both miraculously unhurt, but the stallion proving to be deucedly hard to capture and tie to a tree—she had been promising the good Lord everything she could think of if only He would spare her having the blood of this innocent man on her hands. She would be good, she had vowed on a sob; she would mend her Evil Ways and listen to her papa, who had warned her time and again that one day her little pranks and playful nature would end in disaster. If only the man would be all right, she had bargained fervently, she would nurse him back to health as penance for her sins; all the while being a pattern card of docility and humble contrition.

As if her own fears had not been enough, Lady Penelope had then found herself having to deal with the idiot Benedict butler, Farnley, who had seen her approaching the house at the head of a strange parade that numbered Nemesis and herself, a riderless horse, and a well-dressed but for the moment unconscious gentleman being carried along behind—lying on top of a fence gate balanced between four muscular local farm lads Lady Penelope had spied in a nearby field and hastily commandeered into service.

Farnley, whom she had foolishly assumed would immediately take charge of the situation, had instead shown all the signs of imminent insanity, racing about the foyer wringing his pencil-thin hands and wailing something about a beetle having run across his shoe just that morning in the herb garden, so that he had felt sure there would be a death in the household before evening.

That had left the farm lads—whose brawn seemed not to be limited to their strong backs, but also to exist in ample supply between their freckled, jug-handled ears—to panic, causing them to immediately drop the fence gate and scamper off, while the unconscious gentleman slowly rolled over to land nose down in the mud beside the brick path.

As if that had not been enough (although Lady Penelope was sure she would have been hard-pressed to find anyone in all of the world so mean natured as to believe what she had already suffered was *not* enough), her Aunt Lucinda had then flitted to the open doorway, seen the very still form lying sprawled in the path, screeched, " 'O! woe is me, To have seen what I have seen, see what I see!' Shakespeare," and then promptly fainted into Lady Penelope's startled embrace.

No, all in all, it wasn't exactly the optimum moment for her ungrateful patient to employ sarcasm at her expense. "Oh, do be quiet! You're in no position to be rude," she shot at him huffily, her disdain for all men blinding her temporarily to the fact that this particular man was lying before her injured and helpless. "Who do you think you are, anyway?"

Lucien opened his mouth to tell the lady exactly who he was, a move that should immediately render her speechless (a notion that, considering the aching state of his head, appealed more with each passing moment), but quickly thought better of it. A wise man first scented out the landscape before committing himself to anything. After all, he was in no position to escape wherever he was, and he did not much care to be put at a disadvantage. No, for the time being he would keep his identity his own little secret.

Finally, just as Lady Penelope (who had belatedly remembered that she had promised to be good if only this man's life could be spared) was about to do something quite rare—beg forgiveness for her behavior—Lucien said in what could only be called an apologetic tone: "Could we possibly gnaw on that particular bone at some other time? Pardon me, please, but for the moment that small bit of information seems determined to elude me."

"Ah, sweet Jesus, the poor fella," Doreen Sweeney, overhearing, exclaimed, crossing herself. She had just re-entered the sickroom to report that the doctor—after pouring down two glasses of Mrs. Benedict's small store of port—had gone off to attend the lying-in of Squire Nevin's second-best milk cow. "Doesn't know who he is, does he? You want to know what it was? It was that pop on his noggin what did it, Lady Penelope, sure as check. Do you think he'll be dyin' then?"

Lady Penelope? Lucien marveled, a tingle of apprehension running down his spine. Could this possibly be Philip's Penelope? The "Nose"? Of all the dratted coincidences, this one bears off the palm! His breath hissed audibly through his teeth as Lucien thanked his lucky stars for keeping his counsel about his identity even while he silently cursed Hawkedon for misleading him about his sister's overwhelming good looks.

Lady Penelope quickly put a finger to her lips to silence her maid, who had already blessed herself three times and was now fumbling in her apron pocket for her rosary beads. "He's not going to die, Doreen," she assured her, "unless you've just succeeded in scaring the poor gentleman to death. Now why don't you go downstairs and brew up some of your special tea for our invalid—you say it helps anything."

It was true; Doreen had been plying her specially brewed tea at Weybridge Manor ever since her arrival, lauding its power to reduce swellings, cure headaches, and ease stomach pains better than any medicine. But she was a wise woman, and knew her limitations. "And when did I ever say my tea was a magic potion that could right a scrambled brain?" she prodded, shaking her head. "Lord love a duck, milady, it's more than a few tea leaves that sorry fella's needin'."

Lady Penelope was fast losing her patience. Once more escorting her maid to the door of the chamber, she repeated her suggestion, amending it to include brewing an extra cup of tea for Aunt Lucinda who, as far as Lady Penelope knew, was still lying sprawled on a small divan in her own chambers, mumbling random lines from *Paradise Lost*. "And don't feel you have to hurry back," she ended, just before closing the door and turning the key in the lock.

Doreen meant well, Lady Penelope mused as she turned back to her patient, who was now lying quietly in the bed, his hands curled into tight fists at his sides. He seemed to be all right, but overhearing much more of the maid's concerns might be more than the poor man could handle in his present weakened state. Walking softly across the room to stand beside the high bed, Lady Penelope looked down at her patient assessingly, taking in the fact that the man's toes stretched down the length of the bed under the covers fully a foot more than her own small body would have.

His shoulders, hidden beneath the white lawn nightshirt Doreen had unearthed from the small, wrapped packet one of the servants had detached from the stallion's saddle, were quite broad, definitely more muscular in form than those of her brother Philippos, who had always been the model against whom she had measured all other men.

And he was so dark. His hair, especially now, banded about as it was with the white bandage the doctor had placed there, seemed as dark as a moonless night, and his eyes, what little she had seen of them, reminded her of two chips of hard, black coal. He was five and thirty if he was a day, she decided, still comparing the man to her brother, whom she knew to be a youthful-looking thirty.

No, he was nothing like Philippos or the twins or, for that matter, anyone of her acquaintance. He exuded power, even lying there motionless beneath the covers, and he had the air of one who was used to command. She was convinced he must be feeling absolutely helpless, and his ill humor was clear evidence that he would prove to be a horrible invalid, not that she could find it in her heart to blame him. She should think she'd be even more terrible if their roles were reversed.

So thinking, Lady Penelope reached down to tuck the covers more carefully around the man's injured ribs, saying kindly, "My maid is gone now, sir. I'm sorry if she upset you, but she's Irish, you understand, and prone to indulging in displays of emotion. I notice you haven't said anything in quite some time. I assure you, the doctor has told us you should be fit again very soon, so please don't worry."

"You can have no idea how that piece of information relieves my mind, Lady Penelope," Lucien replied pointedly, reaching up to grab her wrist in his grip. "Please excuse me for my earlier rudeness, ma'am, but I do believe I am not quite myself—whoever that is."

"Oh, no, on the contrary. Please forgive *me*," Lady Penelope apologized, looking down to where Lucien's hand held her. "You've had quite a shock, haven't you. I really can't blame you for being a little out of sorts. Are you quite sure you can't remember your name?"

So this is Philip's little sister, is it? he thought, looking up into Lady Penelope's flushed features. Beautiful she might be, but she has the disposition of a warthog caught in a trap. Lord save me from willful women! Philip should have had no fear of my tumbling into love with the chit.

Philip!

What a damnable mess he had landed himself in this time! If Philip got wind of it, there'd be the devil to pay for sure, with his friend hying himself over here as fast as he could to hurry the romance along, just to ease his own conscience over declaring for Dorinda Redfern. The fellow would be beside himself with glee, knowing he had a captive audience for his schemes. Lucien didn't put it past his friend to even engineer a compromising situation between himself and the beauteous Lady Penelope.

"Sir?" Lady Penelope prompted when Lucien made no reply to her question.

"I'm quite sure I can't remember, ma'am," he lied, lowering his eyelids and trying his best to look pitiful. She had gotten him into this mess, the little minx, and he could see no reason to ease her conscience in the matter. "Perhaps—perhaps if you could tell me how I came to be lying in this bed, and exactly where we are?"

Feeling it prudent to put off the explanation of how he

had come to tumble off his horse until later—when her wrist was no longer within reach of his surprisingly strong hand—Lady Penelope decided to answer the second half of his question first. "You're in my Aunt Lucinda's house, just outside Wormhill, near Buxton, in Derbyshire. That's in England, you know," she added scrupulously. "I don't know what people in your condition can remember."

"Wormhill." He made the name sound like some noxious weed. "Ah, what a poetic name. I must have been passing by to somewhere else. Even if I am not quite sure who I am, I have the distinct feeling I am not someone who would voluntarily be stopping in Wormhill for the Season."

"Not all of us have the option of staying where we will," Lady Penelope shot back, stung. "Besides, it is not such a terrible place. I understand the natives often stay up past their ten o'clock prayers, libertine creatures that they are."

"Then you, too, are a visitor to fair Wormhill?" Oh, yes, this is the "Nose" all right. If nothing else, I've got to admire her spunk.

Lucien's last question brought up memories of the Marquess's parting words to her, words that left Lady Penelope with no illusions as to her fate if she dared to blot her copybook during her sojourn at Lucinda Benedict's. "You might say that," she admitted, finally succeeding in getting back possession of her left wrist and then walking across to the window to look out over the barren garden. "I only arrived today, for a visit that should not extend past the first day of spring. I had thought myself to be utterly bored here in the country, but your unfortunate accident seems to have changed all that. As my aunt, your real hostess, is not quite up to nursing you, sir, I shall be in charge of your recovery. It is only fitting."

My, my sweetings, don't sound so overjoyed. Aloud, he only said, "And that, I believe, brings us back to how I got here. Was there a carriage accident?"

Deliberately keeping her back turned to him, Lady Penelope said shortly, "You took a fall from your horse near here. You have a badly sprained ankle, I'm afraid, as well as a few cracked ribs and that bump on your head. Actually, you should be resting, trying to regain your strength. Your memory will probably come back to you soon enough, so there's really no need to dwell on the details of the accident right now, is there?''

Lucien Kenrick knew a guilty conscience when he heard one, and although he longed to close his eyes and go to sleep, he pushed on, goading Lady Penelope deliberately. ''You perhaps witnessed this accident, ma'am? I am much distressed, and can only hope being told exactly what transpired might jog me into remembering my name. You cannot know how helpless I am feeling at the moment, how cast adrift I imagine myself to be. Please, Lady Penelope. Surely you cannot mean to leave me lying here . . . alone . . . wondering.''

Lady Penelope tried hard—very hard—to count to ten, remembering her promise to be good, but it was not to be. Her guilt (colliding with the sickening realization that she had promised to nurse this infuriating man back to health) goaded her into whirling about to blurt, *''It wasn't all my fault!''*

Leighton turned his head slightly in her direction, to find that the pain of this movement was well worth the sight Lady Penelope presented to his weary eyes. Her long, unbound hair seemed to take on a life of its own as it swirled about her head, and her beautiful, darkly lashed eyes were suddenly two sparkling green pools of liquid emerald.

She was, he decided appreciatively, a completely *female* female—all fire and emotion, and fiercely passionate. ''Your fault?'' he asked, pretending shocked disbelief at her outburst. ''You did this to me?''

''Don't interrupt me!'' she countered, pointing a finger at him in warning. ''It wasn't as if I asked you to race me, for heaven's sake. And then when you didn't rein in as we neared the wall, I thought you must have known the jump was safe, but you didn't, did you?''

''I didn't? How remiss of me.''

''No, you did not! You kept on racing toward the jump anyway, just as if you knew what you were doing, so how was I to know you were just being stupid? And then there was suddenly this hay cart on the other side of the wall, and we both ended by being tossed from the saddle. *I* managed to land without hurting myself. It was only *you* who was so addlepated as to hit your head on the edge of the hay cart.''

"My list of sins grows by the moment. Do you suppose I've suffered enough, or would you rather I'd expired on the instant, thus satisfying your thirst for revenge?'' Clearly Leighton was enjoying himself, and just as clearly Lady Penelope was becoming more incensed.

"How dare you make fun of me!'' she exclaimed. "You can't even begin to imagine the trouble you have been to me ever since your fall, just as if I hadn't enough on my plate as it was—what with Papa's threats—without you coming along to make my life even more complicated. Well, let me tell you, Mister Whatever Your Name Is, I may have to shoulder my share of the blame for your present condition, I may have to nurse you until you discover who you are and are well enough to leave my aunt's household, I may even have to give some consideration to there being the *slight* possibility of some faint sense in my father's warnings, but I want to make one thing perfectly clear to you: I *will not* like it. I will not like it one single bit!''

Leighton found it was now possible to open his eyes completely, a feat he had accomplished only moments after Lady Penelope had first launched into her passionate tirade, finding himself not so injured that he could not appreciate the sight of a handsome woman in full fury.

He continued to watch, entranced, as she unwittingly aided him by filling in the remainder of the puzzle pieces in his mental picture of her present situation. Now—adding what she had told him to what Philip had already supplied—slowly, carefully, a plan began to form in his mind.

Once her outburst was over, she seemed to be totally at a loss as to anything else to say, and only spread her arms wide in an expression of impotence, then fled the room, never seeing the small smile that had formed on Lucien's lips.

"Oh, sweetings,'' he breathed once she was gone, carefully easing himself into a more comfortable position, "you're really in a pickle, aren't you? Poor, headstrong, spoiled infant. I do believe I shall enjoy putting you through a few hoops."

Chapter Six

LADY Penelope dragged her weary body into the sunlit drawing room and collapsed inelegantly into one of the pair of ugly, overly ornate Sheraton chairs. Facing her, her aunt was perched sideways in the chair's mate, her hands lightly caressing the two grotesque carved wooden griffin's heads that served as decorative accents on the back of her chair.

Having now spent nearly three full days in the household and having made the acquaintance of Pansy, Farnley's scatterbrained wife and Aunt Lucinda's housekeeper (of sorts), Lady Penelope had already been warned that these two chairs represented the entire estate of Aunt Lucinda's dear departed husband, Jerome Benedict, and should not be remarked on in any but the most flattering way.

As waxing poetic over the two monstrosities was a feat beyond Lady Penelope's rapidly depleting stores of energy, she had compromised, taking care to sit in the chairs (the one sporting the less lethal-looking camel's heads) as often as possible, thereby showing her appreciation rather than having to voice it. Indeed, she saw her action in the way of a penance—just another serving of sackcloth and ashes to be heaped atop the long list of humiliations she had been forced to suffer thanks to the insufferable invalid now lying in sybaritic comfort upstairs in *her* chamber.

How she rued ever having made that reckless vow to mend her ways if only the Almighty would spare the nameless man who had landed unconscious at her feet the day she had arrived at Wormhill. She should have known her impulsive promise hadn't really been needed; should have realized at first sight that any man as blatantly obnoxious as her patient was entirely too obstinate to expire quietly merely because he had conked his miserable head against a hay cart.

It would take a good deal more to do in such a creature—perhaps even a horde of Furies, she mused evilly, a small anticipatory smile stealing across her features before sliding away.

Not that she really wished him underground, because she didn't. But if she had thought nursing the twins through the measles had been rough going, she now realized it had been a leisurely stroll in the park compared to keeping her current patient amused.

Her head moving side to side wearily, she recited aloud, singsong, " 'Fetch me another blanket, Lady Penelope.' 'This soup seems to have grown cold. Please take it back to the kitchens and reheat it, Lady Penelope.' 'Plump up my pillows, for my head aches abominably, Lady Penelope.' '*Read* to me, Lady Penelope, for time is hanging heavy on my hands.' *Bah!* I'm surprised he hasn't thought to ask me to chew his mutton for him, for heaven's sake!''

" 'Men are but children of a larger growth,' Dryden,'' Aunt Lucinda remarked comfortingly, giving the griffin heads each a last, loving pat and then moving about in her chair in order to face her niece. She carefully pushed at her dyed-blonde ringlets, smoothed down the front of her ruffled crepe gown, and spread her hands regally, palms up, as if inviting Lady Penelope's confidences.

If nothing else, the past three days had taught Lady Penelope that it was possible to converse with her eccentric aunt, even if her penchant for speaking only in quotes had been difficult to comprehend at first. There was actually a lot of wisdom to be found in the lady—although, Lady Penelope had found there was also a surfeit of nonsense to be heard as well—and now she actually found herself looking forward to their strange linguistic interludes.

"How right you are, Aunt," Lady Penelope responded eagerly, nodding her head. "He reminds me of a spoiled, puling infant, never happy unless I am at his constant beck and call. Do you know what he did this morning? He bellowed for me—I cannot think of another word to adequately describe the way he calls for me—not two minutes after I had left the sickroom. When I arrived in his room, out of breath from having run up the stairs—as he knew full well, seeing that I had gone downstairs on an errand for *him*—he had the absolute *gall* to say, 'Lady Penelope, whatever took you so long? Can it be you have tired of playing nursemaid? It's time for my medicine, you know.'

" 'It's sitting right beside you on the table. Surely you are sufficiently recovered to pour your own medicine?' I suggested most kindly, while longing to hold his dratted nose for him and pour the entire contents down his gullet—then follow it with the bottle itself.

"And do you know what he said to me? Oh, you won't believe it, Aunt Lucinda! He lay there all propped against the pillows and whined, 'But it tastes so much better when *you hold the spoon.*' What do you think of that, Aunt?"

The older woman shook her head in commiseration. " 'It beggar'd all description,' Shakespeare."

"Indeed, yes! You cannot imagine how I long to box his ears for him, as I would do with any recalcitrant toddler, but I know that's impossible.

"Not only is there my vow to nurse him if only he should survive his fall—the most ridiculous promise I have ever made, and the one that seems to have been the most needless—but there is also that stupid wager of my Papa's hanging over my head like a sharp sword suspended from a delicate, already fraying thread. Why, if Papa should ever get wind of this last debacle of mine, I'd be on my way to a London Season before I could so much as catch my breath."

Aunt Lucinda, who had heard all of this before, nodded sympathetically, reaching over to squeeze Lady Penelope's hand. " 'When we cannot act as we wish, we must act as we can,' Terence."

"Well, I *have* been good, haven't I, Aunt Lucinda?" Lady Penelope asked, seeking reassurance. "Though I must tell you, I do not believe I was created to be a martyr. But what else can I do?"

" 'We ask advice, but we mean approbation,' Colton," her smiling aunt replied triumphantly, waving one pudgy, beringed finger at her niece.

Lady Penelope's full lower lip jutted forward as she pretended to pout. "And what's wrong with that? I think I deserve a little praise for my absolutely *exemplary* behavior of the past few days. You cannot know what a sad trial being good is for me. You may not believe this, Aunt Lucinda, having never witnessed it, but I can really be *quite awful* when I put my mind to it."

Lucinda, who had committed much of the great bard's works to memory before learning that her benefactress, the dearest Dowager Duchess of Avonall, refused to have his words quoted in her presence ("I will not countenance the wanton bantering about of Shakespeare's immortal words whenever you wish to remark on such subjects as cinch bugs on my roses or the proper time to turn sheets."), was delighted to recite one of her memorized lines now for her niece. " 'What! Canst thou say all this and never blush?' Shakespeare."

Her niece threw back her head and laughed in appreciation of her aunt's wit, but her laughter was cut off abruptly by the impatient ringing of the small silver dinner bell now in the possession of her patient. Her beautiful face taking on a thundercloud aspect, her finely arched brows pressed low on her forehead as her green eyes narrowed to glittering slits, she raised her head and said something very unlovely to the ceiling above her head.

" 'There is, however, a limit at which forbearance ceases to be a virtue,' Burke," Aunt Lucinda prodded softly, winking in her niece's direction.

"You aren't suggesting I ignore his last imperious summons, are you, Aunt?" Lady Penelope bit her lip as she considered Lucinda's—or rather, Edmund Burke's—words. "I have not been out riding on Nemesis since my fall, and it *is* a lovely afternoon, isn't it? But, no. What if he truly needs me? The poor fellow still can't remember his name, and there was nothing to the point about his identity to be found among his personal possessions. He may be feeling low again, and need me to hold his hand. I really shouldn't be thinking of myself, in any case. After all, I did promise—"

" 'A woman's vow I write upon the wave,' Sophocles," Aunt Lucinda quoted, whether to support her niece's planned defection or to censure it, Lady Penelope could not be sure. She looked toward the glass doors leading to the gardens, and a few blessed hours of freedom, then toward the stairway in the foyer—the stairway that would lead her back to her demanding patient.

She couldn't decide, feeling torn by her desire to escape her new responsibilities and her equally strong need to make amends for her former lack of responsible action.

The ringing of the bell came again, louder, longer, and even more insistent, and Lady Penelope leaped to her feet before bending down to give her aunt a kiss on the cheek. "I don't know if you and your friend Sophocles were being facetious or not, Aunt Lucinda, but I must say I do not much care for his low opinion of our gender. Much as I should like to run upstairs, rip that infernal bell out of his hands, and do something very unladylike with it to our resident tyrant, I shall restrain myself, if only for the fact that I refuse to allow a mere man to goad me into breaking a vow I have made."

She turned to leave the room, then swiveled back around to wag her finger at her aunt as she added, "But he can raise the hackles on my back more than any one person I have ever met, and he'd be wise to make a miraculous recovery and quit this place soon, for I don't believe I shall be able to endure this much longer without doing *something* terrible!"

Lucinda Benedict watched as Lady Penelope scampered out of the room, skirts held high above her slim, well-turned ankles as the young woman made her way to the stairway, then she turned once more in her chair to stroke one of the griffin heads reflectively as she looked up at the ceiling and directed what could be either a compliment or a warning to her injured guest, " 'That's a valiant flea that dare eat his breakfast on the lip of a lion,' Shakespeare."

Lucien stopped ringing the silver bell long enough to place a hand on his ear and listen for sounds in the hallway outside his door. "Ah," he breathed after a moment, amused, "methinks I hear the gentle footfalls of my nurse. I do so love a woman who knows her place."

Leighton, sitting comfortably propped up against half a dozen soft feather pillows—and with his injured right ankle resting on three more—was feeling rather full of himself, as he had been for nearly two entire days now, thanks to the rapid healing of his normally disgustingly healthy body and his thorough enjoyment in putting Lady Penelope Rayburn through her paces as his personal lackey.

While he privately acknowledged that what he was doing was not exactly cricket, he was firmly convinced that he deserved at least a small measure of repayment for having been injured in a vain attempt to save the firebrand's beautiful, slim neck. The fact that Lady Penelope was so obvious in showing him that it galled her no end to have found herself in the position of his nurse only added to his enjoyment.

Besides, Lady Penelope Rayburn was quite beautiful—nothing like the woman her brother Philip had erroneously described, for some reason Lucien could not fathom—and he thoroughly enjoyed her company. As long as he was forced to convalesce in a benighted hole like Wormhill, he was entitled to some entertainment.

The door to the room fairly flew open, and Lady Penelope, reminding Lucien of a fresh spring breeze, blew briskly into the room, a set expression on her face. She stopped after having taken only two steps into the chamber, her left hand still holding fast to the doorknob so as to keep the heavy door from slamming against the wall, and took several deep, steadying breaths while she glared at the dark-haired man in the bed.

"Ah, there you are at last," Leighton remarked silkily. "You certainly took your time answering my summons. I do hope I'm not being too much of a bother."

"What is it this—I mean, is there a problem, sir? You've already finished your luncheon, and Pansy did take such care to slice your ham into the thin slivers you desired. Perhaps you want Farnley?" she ended with a patently false show of concern, knowing that she was skirting propriety by referring to his possible need for physical relief.

"*Nobody* wants Farnley, Lady Penelope," Lucien responded grittily, "unless that body harbors a death wish. The man reminds me of nothing more than a carrion crow, constantly hovering about atop my bedpost, either portending or awaiting disaster."

64

"He is a bit superstitious," Lady Penelope owned, trying to look concerned. "Poor thing, it has made him rather dour, don't you think?"

"On the contrary, I think the fellow enjoys himself immensely. Did you know he wanted to string a garter of *corks* 'round my leg to keep me from getting another cramp like the one I had last night? When I refused—heathen unbeliever that I am—he stuck bunches of huge corks between the mattress and the bed frame at each corner, knowing I couldn't stop him, and then ran out. Now I can't sleep, and I'm convinced it's because the mattress is uneven. Can't you do something about that man? I need my rest if I'm ever to remember who I am."

Remembering how she had been rudely roused from a deep sleep the night before by the sound of her patient's passionate curses as his leg had been seized in a painful cramp, and how she had spent nearly half an hour rubbing that same patient's knotted calf just as if he were some prized bit of horseflesh and she were his groom, Lady Penelope tilted her head to one side, actually considering whether or not, in this particular case, Farnley's admittedly farfetched application of superstitious nonsense might just have some merit.

"Perhaps," she said at last, "you ought to allow the corks to remain. Just for one night, you understand, as a sort of test. After all, Farnley seems fairly knowledgeable about these things."

"Oh, really," the Earl said, rolling his dark eyes.

"Yes, really. Why, just this morning, while she was preparing your luncheon tray, Pansy told me how she had accidently dropped a spoon on the kitchen table at breakfast three days ago and Farnley had immediately jumped up to declare that a visitor would arrive before nightfall. And you did, didn't you?"

Lucien shook his head in wry amusement. "I did, didn't I? However, Lady Penelope—and please forgive me for pointing out the obvious—so did *you*, if I recall what you have told me correctly. Farnley already knew that you had been expected, didn't he?"

Lady Penelope pulled a face. "That charlatan!" she exclaimed, shaking her head. "Now why on earth did he do that, do you suppose?"

"I imagine he was just showing off for his impressionable wife, but if you, too, care to fall in with such nonsense, you certainly have my permission, for I know how you ladies love your little myths. I, however, harbor no such faith in Farnley's ability to foretell anything more weighty than whether or not, in his opinion, next spring's grass will be green! No, ma'am, I repeat, the corks must go. Now." Lucien's words, though softly spoken, were a definite demand for service.

Lady Penelope took another step into the room and turned around, grabbing the edge of the door in her right hand in preparation of slamming it shut with all her might. She then thought better of the action and merely closed the door with a carefully controlled whisper of sound that should have alerted Leighton to the existence of the dangerous cauldron full of repressed anger that bubbled just behind her forced façade of concern (a pot already loaded with the indignation that had been simmering ever since she had first been told she must spend the winter at Wormhill, and added to daily since his advent into her life), ready to boil over if he added just one more drop of provocation.

But the Earl, unheeding, opened his mouth yet again— pettishly warning her to be careful not to jostle his poor, aching body as she executed his command—thereby presenting Lady Penelope with the final ingredient that was all that was needed to send her cascading over the edge and into direct action.

Turning again to face him, she nodded as if in answer to some silent question she had asked herself, and then approached the bed, a small smile playing about the corners of her mouth. Looking him square in the eyes, she bent down slightly and lifted the corner of the mattress that lay just below his injured ankle. Up, up, she hoisted the mattress, straining against its weight as he smiled at her benignly, before she succeeded in extracting one of the large brown corks Farnley had slipped onto the frame.

Raising the cork in one hand, she displayed it for Lucien's benefit and gave him a thin smile as he praised her in much the way one would reward a faithful hound who had just fetched his master's slippers. "Whoops, I think I'm going to be clumsy," she said after a moment, deadpan, her smile disappearing as the light of battle flashed in her narrowed green eyes. A moment later, just as the helpless Lucien belatedly realized what she was about to do, she abruptly let go of the mattress, causing it to drop sharply back down onto the frame.

"*Ouch!* Damn it, woman, you did that on purpose!" Lucien shouted, quickly reaching down with both hands to hold onto his injured leg.

Lady Penelope was instantly contrite. She had tried so hard to be good, but she seemed to be fighting a losing battle. She was just as willful and dangerously playful as her father said she was. Would she never learn? Rushing to stand beside the head of the bed, she leaned over her latest victim, all womanly concern. "Does it hurt badly?" she asked hurriedly. "I'm so very sorry! I don't know what got into me, really I don't. I'm not usually purposely cruel. It's just that—"

She never got to finish her apology, as Lucien let go of his two-fisted grip on his knee and reached up to haul Lady Penelope unceremoniously across his stomach, her startled face now only inches from his own. Her long redgold hair, which was hanging loose past her shoulders behind a simple headband, splayed out over the coverlet, a few of the fiery curls tangling across Lucien's features like spun, carmelized sugar. Her arms, pinned to her sides, lent her no support, and her feet dangled awkwardly a full three feet above the floor.

She was startled into silence, oddly breathless and totally helpless.

She was just where Lucien Kenrick wanted her—had wanted her ever since he first caught sight of her riding that great grey gelding three days earlier.

The throbbing ache in his ankle was as less than nothing to him, the soreness of his ribs a mere irritation easily to be borne. He had a lapful of warm, soft female, and he was not about to let a trifling thing like physical pain deter him from the path he had chosen.

He raised his head slowly, not knowing how rakishly

handsome he looked, his dark hair curling on the wide white bandage, and examined the small, wide-eyed face that was so close to his.

The clean, perfumed scent of her just-washed hair teasing his nostrils, he marveled at the exquisite fineness of her pale skin, the way the soft flush on her cheeks so accented her darkly lashed, emerald green eyes.

And her mouth—those full, pouting, pink lips that had been set in such a thin, tightly controlled line as she had tried to hold back her less than gentle temper while he had goaded her mercilessly for two days—drew his eager gaze even while his tongue moved provocatively against the back of his teeth, already contemplating what it would be like to taste her honeyed sweetness.

His inventory of her charms, which did not overlook the heady sensations brought on by the weight of her soft body as it nestled so intimately against his chest and thighs, convinced him that he was holding a woman who had been born to be a man's possession, a creature who had been perfectly fashioned to be a man's delight.

What a waste, the world would say, that she had vowed never to wed. But, his self-serving inner voice whispered silently, as he, too, had vowed to remain unwed, it seemed a bleeding pity that both of them should forego the single pleasure the married state could sometimes bring, in order to avoid all the pain of legal bondage.

Physical pleasure.

This soothing of his conscience took but a few seconds, for he had no intention of allowing such an opportune moment to slip by without taking advantage of it, and he raised his gaze to Lady Penelope's eyes, staring at her meaningfully as slowly, inexorably, he drew her closer.

He could see the indecision in her eyes, and delighted in the way her gaze flitted nervously away from his, moving down to his slightly open mouth before returning once more to frown at him in mingled interest and confusion.

For she was feeling it, too—this sudden intense physical attraction to each other, this crackling field of pure energy that held them both in thrall.

It's a healthy young kitten the dear Lady Penelope is,

Leighton told himself reassuringly—brave and willing to risk danger to satisfy its natural curiosity.

"Come here, little puss," he breathed softly, his mouth now hovering a scant inch above hers. "Let me hear you purr."

Lady Penelope had once seen her brother Philippos lying in the soft grass behind the dairy with Dorcas, the Weybridge upstairs maid, doing something much like she was about to do with her handsome patient. At the time, the intense expression on Philippos's face had seemed comic, almost laughable. Yet that same expression had an extremely different effect on her now, as she saw it mirrored in Lucien's dark features.

Maybe it was because *she* was now the cause of that strange, disquieting look; she, and not the silly, ample-hipped Dorcas, who *had* giggled at poor Philippos behind the dairy. Lady Penelope knew she could never be as heartless as the maid had been. Perhaps it was because she had the niggling suspicion that her own face was also wearing much the same, odd expression.

She certainly *felt* intense. Intense and strangely fluttery, and—oddly enough—almost hungry.

Then his lips were on hers, and the time for thinking was over. Now there was time only for sensation.

Blue, her body whispered to her softly, our whole being feels blue. Feel it. Midnight blue—like the deep, dark waters of some bottomless ocean. And now the red. Feel the curving waves of intense, velvety red, stroking hidden shores deep inside us; and the small, hot circles of brightest yellow, like a hundred miniature suns exploding one by one above it all in their glory, each brilliant burst growing larger and more intense than the last.

Her body was confused, not knowing if it was thirsty or made up entirely of liquid. Her skin was at once a heaven and a prison, tingling with pleasure yet not allowing her the closeness she suddenly craved more than the air she gulped deep into her lungs. His mouth had left hers to plant a row of tiny kisses down the side of her throat, sowing seeds of desire that grew quickly into softly petaled flowers that he seemed to be plucking even as they burst into bloom.

The kiss had answered many of the questions she had longed to ask Philippos, but left her with another new set of vaguely embarrassing questions that rudely shook her back to reality.

And that reality told her she was lying on top of an injured stranger, a man who was at that very moment indulging himself in a way that no well-bred young lady should allow—for even motherless Lady Penelope was not so uneducated as to think what had just occurred between her and the heavily-breathing man beneath her was within the realm of social acceptability. Her only thought now was of escape—an escape that would leave her few remaining shreds of pride intact.

If he had meant to humiliate her, he had certainly accomplished his aim. She would rather he had treated her like the child she had acted and spanked her. This punishment, she knew instinctively, would remain in her mind longer than any spanking ever could.

Feeling Lady Penelope's body growing stiff and still beneath his hands, Lucien opened his eyes to stare sightlessly over her narrow shoulder at the ugly oak armoire across the room, wondering just when his little exercise in educating her had turned into an unlooked-for lesson in humility for him. It wasn't that he had expected their kiss to leave him unmoved; Lady Penelope was far too intriguing, too beautiful, to either bore or repulse him. He had known she would please him.

But he hadn't expected to be shaken down to his toes with his own sanity-stripping response to her innocently passionate reaction. After all, he'd held many a warm, willing woman in his arms.

You just didn't think this thing through before you acted, Leighton, that's all. All right, he concluded, better late than never. Start thinking.

Perhaps it was just that she was a warm, willing *virgin* who had all but knocked him into horsetails? Heaven knew it was a new experience for him. It had obviously been a new experience for her, too, and much more of a lesson than he had intended when first the idea had crept into his head.

So now what was he supposed to do?

If Philip Rayburn ever gets wind of this little episode, friend or not, he'll have my liver and lights for certain— right after the wedding ceremony, that is. For one fleeting moment Lucien felt his body tense, just as if he were about to fling Lady Penelope away from him so that he could run off to the wilds of Scotland to hide until the Marquess of Weybridge had his hoydenish daughter safely bracketed to some nice safe Viscount or something.

Just as quickly, he relaxed, realizing that the Marquess, just like Lady Penelope, had no idea who he was and would think he himself had no idea of his own identity.

You're thinking all right, Leighton—conniving like some out and out cad, he told himself, halting that particular train of thought. You wanted to kiss the lady, you saw your opportunity, and you gave in to the impulse—that's the beginning, the middle, and the end of it. It was a one time thing, a temporary aberration, and if you don't do anything stupid in the next few minutes, the entire episode will be quickly forgotten.

Unless you've suddenly taken some insane notion to stick your neck back inside the parson's mousetrap, an inner voice suggested facetiously. Oh no, not me, he protested quickly, already pushing Lady Penelope away from her resting place against his shoulder. Once bitten, twice shy, as the saying goes. I'll never marry again.

Lucien's lack of further assault on her senses finally allowing her to recover her powers of concentration, Lady Penelope abruptly found herself struggling to cover the awkwardness of finding herself seated bolt upright on Lucien's lap while the two of them studiously ignored each other. Why is he feeling uncomfortable? Was kissing me that repugnant to him?

The silence grew until the clock on the mantelpiece struck the hour of four, startling Lady Penelope into action.

"No wonder Dorcas is always smiling," she blurted, in aid of nothing, then gave out an awkward giggle while inwardly deciding she could actually see the solid wall of mutual apprehension that had sprung up between them.

"What?" Lucien questioned blankly, knowing that, of

all the many things she could have said, Lady Penelope was remaining an Original to the end. "Who's Dorcas?"

Lady Penelope slapped a hand to her mouth, unable to believe she had said anything quite so silly. "I, er, it was nothing. Just something I—never mind," she said, moving her head about almost frantically, trying in vain to figure out a way to get herself down from her perch without having her hands come into any further contact with his body. "Please excuse me now," she mumbled as she began slowly easing her toes toward the floor.

She attributed Lucien's expression of pain to the continued pressure of her body against his still-tender ribs, and he did not bother to correct her misconception, wishing as fervently as she to have their more intimate contact broken as quickly as possible. Raising his tortured gaze to the ceiling, he concentrated on forming some reasonable explanation for his disgraceful behavior and tried with all his might not to notice the awkward, intimate placement of her hands as she struggled to stand up.

"I—I have to go now. I believe Farnley will be stopping by soon to help you, um, prepare for your dinner," Lady Penelope stammered once she was safely back on the floor, self-consciously straightening her twisted gown. "I promise you there will be no repeat of my childish pranks. You have punished me enough."

Is that how you wish to think about our recent activity? As a sort of punishment? Very well, minx. I may not be the perfect gentleman, but I will bow to your wishes. Aloud, Lucien only said, "I should certainly hope so, Lady Penelope. Since my memory has failed me, I can only say that I cannot recall the last time I resorted to taking physical action against a female, but I can't believe that I am usually so brutish a creature. It must be my injuries—and my inability to remember who I am. I tell you, Lady Penelope, you can have no idea how adrift I feel; just as if I had been cast overboard, into a wide, dark blue ocean."

Blue.

Midnight blue.

"Oh!" It was a low, involuntary cry, thin, like a small

72

creature in pain, and Lucien quickly turned his head to look at Lady Penelope, concern evident in his dark eyes.

Unable to stay in the room any longer without bursting into embarrassed tears, Lady Penelope, her small face suddenly colorless inside her tangled curtain of red-gold curls, whirled on her toes and sped out of the room.

She left a thoroughly shaken Lucien Kenrick behind to stare after her, wondering why he wished Farnley would appear so that he could ask the man to drop something very heavy on his injured ankle.

Chapter Seven

LADY Penelope had studiously avoided her patient for the remainder of the day before spending a rare, sleepless night wherein she endlessly relived the shattering interlude she had experienced in his arms. Although the troubled young woman finally did fall into a light, restless slumber an hour before dawn, Doreen had no trouble awakening her mistress for her morning chocolate just as the large, ornate Thomas Johnson anti-Gallic clock in the upstairs hallway wheezed out the hour of nine.

"Your young man is up and callin' for you already, milady," Doreen informed Lady Penelope even as she grudgingly held open the bedroom door to allow Farnley to enter, the butler laboriously carrying a heavy bucket of hot water that he promptly poured into the small, steep-sided bathtub already in position before the fireplace.

"Oh?" Lady Penelope responded in a belligerent tone, wondering why her stomach insisted upon doing a little flip inside her. "Did he by any chance tell you what he wants? I don't care how ill he is, I shall not hold his tooth cup for him while he snorts and spits."

"Glory, milady, it's nothing like that. He says he has a surprise for you. Maybe he's about to try his legs, I'm thinkin', and it would be a good turn to us all if he did. You're lookin' sorta peaky this mornin', truth to tell. The man's runnin' you ragged. Here now, Farnley, and look how you're sloppin' water all over that fine rug! Have a care!"

"There's nothing to worry about, if you don't mind my saying so," the butler told Doreen as he spilled the last of the steaming liquid into the tub. "This here's rainwater.

74

The only time spilled water means bad luck is if it's water pulled from a well or pool.''

"Well then," Doreen replied consideringly, "doesn't that make me feel ten kinds of a fool for yellin' at you. Tell me, Farnley, would you be thinkin' havin' your head bashed in by my dear departed da's shillelagh to be a bit of bad luck, you scrawny, misbegotten scarecrow? I do believe it can be arranged, don't you know.''

Farnley drew himself up to his full height—which was, unfortunately for his opinion of his own consequence, not very impressive—and said repressively, "If ever you should wish water for bathing put in your room, be warned that I shall see that it is first *boiled,* so that the Devil will heap misfortune on you. He will, too, even you ignorant boglanders should know that!''

"Oh, is that the way of it, you snivelin' weasel? It's a good skelping you need, I say," Doreen retorted, one hand raised threateningly as she advanced toward the butler, who was rapidly backing toward the door, as he had already realized that his mouth had somehow outrun his small store of courage. "Ah, thinkin' better of it, are you?" Seeing Farnley in full retreat, she waved her apron at him as she pretended to shoo him out the door. "That's it. Away with you now, little man. Run as quick as you can, and if you fall, don't wait to get up!''

The sound of Lady Penelope's delighted laughter caused Doreen to turn her head and look at her mistress. "Well, and that's better now. Nothin' like a bit of foolery to put the bloom back in those pretty cheeks, don't you know.''

It wasn't until her breakfast of eggs and country ham was eaten and her morning bath completed that Lady Penelope found the courage to ask, "You said my patient has a surprise for me. Did you see him yourself, or did Farnley pass on the message?''

Doreen swore softly under her breath as she realized she had somehow missed one of the small button loops on Lady Penelope's gown, and she busily began unbuttoning the gown back to the point where she had made her mistake—which may have been why her usually finely attuned ears did not pick up the unusual quiver of nervousness that had slipped into her mistress's voice.

"Doreen? Did you hear me?" Lady Penelope prompted after a moment, fidgeting a bit and making the maid's job even more difficult.

"It's cowhanded I'm bein' this mornin', milady, not deaf. Of course I heard you. Just like I heard the mister yellin' at me through the half-closed door like he did. If you want to know what I think, I think the rascal's pilin' it on a bit deep. Such a mess of grandeur he is, lyin' there. He should be up and about by now, not makin' you play fetch and carry all the day long. It ain't fittin'. Now, just let me fix your hair."

Lady Penelope gave a deep, resigned sigh. So much for thinking her patient had suffered as she had over their little interlude. She should have expected as much—after all, he was a *man,* wasn't he?

"Don't bother with anything fancy this morning, Doreen," Lady Penelope said, anxious to get to her patient's room and hear whatever it was he wanted to tell her. "We can just tie it back with a ribbon."

"Praise the saints, milady, what a mess this is and no mistake! Was it sleepin' on your head you were about last night? Don't you go makin' great bones about it if this hurts a bit," she ended, picking up a brush.

While Lady Penelope endured Doreen's tortures with the comb and brush, Lucien Kenrick waited most impatiently in the chamber down the hall, rehearsing the little speech that would dig him deeper into the pit of lies that had begun to yawn wide in front of him the moment he had opened his eyes and spied out the young woman whose overwhelming beauty had lured him into this imbroglio in the first place.

He wasn't feeling particularly proud of himself at the moment, but he had spent half the night cudgeling his brain for a solution that would save both her pride and his skin, and this halfway measure was the best thing he had come up with, the only salvation he could see as long as his injured ankle kept him a prisoner at Wormhill.

There was a slight movement near the open doorway. " 'I am his Highness's dog at Kew; Pray tell me, sir, whose dog are you?' Pope."

These words, spoken in the innocent, singsong voice of

a very young child, startled Lucien out of his brown study, and he looked toward the doorway to see the small figure of an elderly woman, vaguely draped in miles of filmy, flounced pink fabric, standing just inside the room, her curly blonde head tilted inquiringly to one side as she gaily waved one pudgy hand in his direction.

Lucien instinctively pulled the bedcovers higher against his chest. Just as he opened his mouth to ask why in blazes he hadn't been informed that there was to be a visitor from Bedlam dropping by Wormhill this morning, Farnley—who was never far away, it seemed, when there was the chance of anything interesting taking place—inserted his skinny frame into the room.

He drew himself up into a ludicrous parody of attention, then announced in stentorian tones, "This lady here is Mrs. Lucinda Benedict, sir, Lady Penelope's aunt and your hostess, if you don't mind my saying so." He clapped his heels together sharply and turned toward his employer before continuing, "Ma'am, the gentleman does not know whose dog he, er, that is, the gentleman still does not remember who he is."

Leighton prudently bit on his knuckles to keep from laughing out loud.

Aunt Lucinda slowly turned her head to look at Farnley, the man the dear Dowager Duchess of Avonall had the supreme nastiness to send along from London to run the household at Wormhill while her cousin was in residence, and pointed out carefully, " 'One eye of the master sees more than four of the servant's,' Italian Proverb."

"Ma'am?" Farnley asked, for as much as he was around Mrs. Benedict, he had the Devil's own time understanding every second word she said. He'd worked up a potion once, drinking it down precisely at midnight of the first full moon of the summer in the hope he would then be gifted with the ability to read her mind, but it hadn't worked—except to have him visiting the necessary house hourly for three days. Her latest utterance now left him standing in the middle of the bedroom, totally confused.

"I believe Mrs. Benedict is telling you that your explanation was unnecessary, that she already knows of my current, lamentable condition. However, Farnley, I thank you for that sterling introduction. It was truly first-rate. And although I have heard about Mrs. Benedict, I have not before now had the chance to thank her in person for her kind hospitality. You may safely retire now, I think.''

The butler looked closely at the man lying in the bed, as if deciding whether or not to withdraw and leave his mistress there alone with him. After all, it didn't take a large intellect to tell that the dear lady *was* a bit queer in the attic, and she might just send the poor injured fellow toppling into a decline with some of her silly sayings. ''Well, now, I don't know about that, sir, if you don't mind my saying so. Mayhap Mrs. Benedict should come back later when Lady Penelope is here to—'' he began falteringly, only to be cut off by Aunt Lucinda's none too gentle tap between his skinny shoulder blades.

Really, the man was becoming an absolute pest. Perhaps she wouldn't send the Dowager Duchess that nice sampler she had been working on this age, the one that said '' 'Caesar had his Brutus; Charles the First his Cromwell; and George the Third may profit by their example,' Patrick Henry.'' Aunt Lucinda did not exactly know what it meant, but the Dowager had long been an admirer of King George, and she was sure the sampler would please her. '' 'Go and tell those who have sent you that we are here by the will of the nation and that we shall not leave save at the point of bayonets,' Comte De Mirabeau,'' Aunt Lucinda declared with a defiant toss of her drooping curls once she was sure her repeated jabs had succeeded in attracting the butler's attention.

Farnley didn't take more than a moment to decide that he had been wrong—that the best possible thing the patient could have would be a long, uninterrupted interview with the so intelligent Mrs. Benedict—and he quickly backed himself out of the room, anxious to rush down to the kitchens and his dearest wife, Pansy, who was the sole person in the world who truly appreciated him.

But Farnley did feel sorry for the stranger—who certainly couldn't know what he was letting himself in for if Mrs. Benedict was in the mood for a comfortable coze—and as he made his way down the rear staircase, the butler decided to have Pansy make up some special treat for the poor man's dinner. "I could sprinkle a bit of dried poppy petals into a finely spiced rabbit stew without his noticing it," he mused aloud. "That should give him a good night's rest and keep him from running entirely mad with brain fever if Mrs. Benedict stays too long."

While Farnley was on his way to his private pantry to seek out the jar of opium-laden poppy, Leighton was smiling appreciatively at his unexpected guest. Motioning for her to sit herself down in the comfortable though homely, armless conversation chair Lady Penelope had earlier positioned on the window side of his bed, he complimented her on her routing of the sad-faced butler, saying, "Bravo! Well done, Mrs. Benedict. I only wish I could do without the man myself. Not that I haven't tried, you understand, but so far Farnley has been all but oblivious of my desire for privacy. If only I could snap my fingers and be completely healed."

Carefully arranging her trailing skirts about her as she lowered herself into the chair, Aunt Lucinda smiled at him reassuringly and offered, " 'Rome was not built in one day,' Heywood."

What an odd, entertaining nodcock, Lucien thought, grinning back at the woman. How Brummell would have loved her. "Too true, madam," he replied, relaxing his guard. "But I have made great strides since I first arrived so rudely on your doorstep, haven't I? I promise to remember your words and be more patient."

Aunt Lucinda looked into Lucien's dark eyes for a long, measuring minute, then tested the waters by saying in a deceptively pleasant voice, " 'We may with advantage at times forget what we know,' Publicius Syrus."

Leighton stared at Aunt Lucinda, his thoughts tumbling over themselves as a faint niggle of fear tugged at the corners of his mind. *What is she talking about? She looks at me as if she suspects me of something. Could she know who I am? Ridiculous! Impossible! If she did, surely she would have told Lady Penelope by now—wouldn't she? After all, she can't know that I'm shamming it—she'd have to think she was doing me a large favor by telling me who I am. I don't like this. I thought I was the only one running a rig around here. Well, there's only one way to find out!*

"I was speaking only of my frustration at the slowness of my physical recovery, madam," he began, picking his way carefully. "I am not the sort to be lying around idle. You see, I did awake just this morning remembering who I am. I cannot tell you how amazed I was. You cannot imagine how worried I was that I could have been an awful person—perhaps even a hardened criminal—someone who could have started up one night and murdered you all in your beds. Surely that possibility had occurred to you, as you are all women, with only Farnley as protection?"

Aunt Lucinda just shrugged, dismissing such useless conjecture. " 'Cleopatra's nose, had it been shorter, the whole face of the world would have been changed,' Pascal."

Lucien shook his head in wry amusement, bowing to the strange wisdom in Aunt Lucinda's curiously applicable declaration. "You're right, of course, dear madam. What is the sense of thinking about what could or might have been? And especially now, now that I *do* remember everything. I can scarcely wait for Lady Penelope to arrive, so that I can at last tell her my name. She has been feeling so guilty, you know, believing that she is to blame for the state I am in at the moment. I am almost embarrassed at the magnitude of her kind attentions." Lucien wisely stopped talking once he realized he was babbling, wondering if he had overplayed his hand. It wouldn't do to change overnight from a demanding tyrant into a fawning sycophant.

Aunt Lucinda reached over and gently patted the Earl's hand in warning. " 'He who has not a good memory, should never take upon him the trade of lying,' Montaigne," she quoted ominously, causing Leighton to shiver, as if a goose had just run over his grave.

He took recourse in nervous laughter. For as quaintly shatter brained as he was sure she could be in many areas, the old widget's mind seemed to be as sharp as needles when it came to him. "I always liked Montaigne, Mrs. Benedict, but I vow, I fail to see his use in this instance."

She didn't answer, just rose to her feet, wiping her hands together briskly before turning to leave the room. She had heard her niece approaching down the hallway, Lady Penelope's usually brisk steps dragging slightly, as if delaying the inevitable.

The time had come for all good aunts to withdraw to a safe distance—although still within earshot—where she could listen as the Earl of Leighton disclosed his true identity to the young lady Aunt Lucinda had chanced to see clutched in his passionate embrace just a day earlier—Not that she would ever mention such a thing to anybody!

There was really no need for her to stay in the room, for Aunt Lucinda already knew who her unexpected guest was and had known since that first evening when she had peeked into the sickroom when no one was looking, but she had held her own counsel, emulating Syrus, who had warned: "Never thrust your own sickle into another's corn."

She wasn't sure why she had not at one point during the next three days scribbled down the Earl's name on a slip of paper and handed it to her niece; she only knew that she had smelled a rat the moment Farnley had told her their patient could not remember who he was or how he had come to fall off his horse.

If she had learned nothing else during her sojourn in the Duke of Avonall's household, she had learned that nothing was ever exactly as it seemed—not when the more tender emotions entered the picture.

"Wise men say nothing in dangerous times," Seldon had written (and Aunt Lucinda had committed to memory); and some niggling little bit of feminine intuition had whispered in her ear that these were dangerous times indeed.

And so it was that even as Lucien called after her, asking her to stay, Aunt Lucinda floated out of the room, only nodding pleasantly to Lady Penelope as she went, and then closed the door to within a narrow crack before unashamedly listening to the conversation that had begun on the other side.

"You wished to see me?" Lady Penelope was saying just as Aunt Lucinda shooed away a curious housemaid who was standing in the hallway, her arms full of clean bed linens, gawking at her eavesdropping mistress. Aunt Lucinda pressed an ear against the slight opening, eager not to miss a single word of Leighton's sure-to-be-enlightening recitation.

"Yes, Lady Penelope," Lucien began hurriedly, not able to look her directly in the eyes. Lord, but she's beautiful! I'd best get over this rough ground as quickly as possible, before I lose my resolve. "I have a grand piece of news for you. It would seem that I have remembered who I am."

Lady Penelope's heart began pounding hurtfully against her ribs. After being in such a rush to hear what he had to say, she had begun having second thoughts as she walked down the corridor to his room. Now she wished she had never answered his summons at all.

"You have?" she asked him unnecessarily, knowing she must look dreadfully pale. "How very fortunate for you. Perhaps you can now give me the name of someone we can contact. After all, there must be someone worrying about you."

Here I go, Lucien sighed inwardly, crossing his fingers beneath the coverlet. "I imagine you could direct any correspondence to Annabel, in Surrey."

"Annabel?" Lady Penelope asked, swallowing hard. "Is that—I mean, could she be . . . do you mean . . . "

Lucien's dark face took on a sadly solemn expression as he nodded slowly, saying, "My wife, yes. I'm—I'm so sorry."

"You—your wife?" Lady Penelope's voice cracked as she forced herself to remain upright, longing as she was to swoon dead away onto the carpet. How dare he say he's sorry! I don't want to hear that now. He can't be any sorrier than I am. After all, he didn't kiss a married man!

His eyes staring holes in the coverlet, Leighton pushed on relentlessly, knowing he was absolutely the most miserable, mean-spirited creature on the entire earth. "Yes. She and the children must be quite worried about me by now."

"You—your *children!*" Lady Penelope squeaked, tottering across the room to sit down in the chair her Aunt Lucinda had just vacated. This last bit of information passed beyond the realm of belief. "You have *children?*"

Out in the hallway, her expression one of extreme consternation, Aunt Lucinda had recourse in the Bible, quoting softly: " 'Many have fallen by the edge of the sword, but not many as have fallen by the tongue,' Ecclesiasticus.''

"Three," the Earl pursued doggedly, wishing he had never embarked upon this new deception, but powerless to stop it now that it had begun. "Miranda, Gilbert, and little Sedgwick. He's just turned three, you know."

"No, no I didn't know," Lady Penelope answered absently, overcome by shame. She had kissed a married man. Worse, she had dreamt about him, reliving those glorious moments spent in his arms. She had, fool that she was, even begun to spin daydreams about her handsome, anonymous patient. Contrary to everything she had always thought, everything she had ever believed, she had begun entertaining the idea that *this* man was somehow different. Difficult, yes. Demanding in the extreme. But still different—perhaps even equal to her in the strength of his personality.

But she had been wrong; dreadfully, horrendously, *scandalously* wrong. He was married. He wasn't for her; never had been for her. Now there was the faceless Annabel to consider—and little Sedgwick. He even sounded different since he had regained his memory. He sounded . . . *married.* Oh, she was so ashamed, so dreadfully ashamed!

"You haven't asked my name yet, Lady Penelope," Lucien remarked, interrupting her thoughts in order to continue his lie. "I'm Kendall, Lucas Kendall. I'm attached to the Foreign Office in a very minor way. I was on my way north to visit my brother; his wife has just given birth to twins. Thankfully, I had planned my visit to be a surprise, so Theo has no reason for alarm. He has enough on his hands as it is, doesn't he?"

"Uh-huh," Lady Penelope said automatically, still wondering how she would ever be able to look at this man again and not remember how his mouth had felt against hers, how his hands had felt as they roamed her body. "Shall I get you pen and paper so that you can write to Annabel—to your wife, Mr. Kendall? Or would you rather

I wrote the letter? I could assure her of your rapid recovery.''

Lucien looked over at the top of Lady Penelope's downcast head, longing to reach out and gather her into his arms and tell her it was all a lie—a crazy, impetuous, self-serving lie. But no, it was better this way. Look what giving in to his last impulse had done for him. If he had harbored any lingering misgivings as to the wisdom of his actions, the look on the young woman's face as she had absorbed his news had told him better than anything that, no matter how much she had tried to hide the fact, her reaction to his embrace yesterday was only a small taste of the passion of which she was capable.

If she, Philip's only sister, were to tumble into love with him, it would be the worst disaster in the world, for he could not find it in himself to hurt her. He had to put her at a distance and then keep her there until his dratted ankle was fit enough to travel. She made him feel weak, tested his determination to remain heart-whole, and the sooner he was atop Hades and on his way out of her life, the sooner he would be able to remember his determination to love many but be true to none.

''I believe I should like to write the letter myself, Lady Penelope, if you don't mind,'' he replied at last, still looking at the small, dejected figure sitting slumped in the chair. ''After all, it's a bit personal, isn't it?''

The fiery blonde head nodded yet again, and then Lady Penelope rose slowly to her feet, heading for the relative safety of the hallway. ''I'll see to it that pen and paper are brought up to you directly, Mr. Kendall. Perhaps I should have a note sent 'round to the doctor, telling him as well. He had told me that it should only be a matter of time before your past came back to you. If you'll excuse me now, I have to go inform my aunt that you have regained your memory. I'm sure she'll be just as pleased as I am.''

Lucien didn't bother to tell her that her aunt already knew of his miraculous ''recovery,'' although she hadn't stayed long enough to hear his name, but the thought of Lucinda Benedict and the strange, knowing look in her watery blue eyes as she had walked out of the room earlier, reminded him of his misgivings about the lady. "Your aunt," he called out to Lady Penelope's departing back, "is she as learned as she seems? I must say, I was very impressed with her. She certainly has a wide and varied knowledge of literature."

Lady Penelope turned back to smile weakly at Lucien. "Aunt Lucinda? Learned? According to Farnley, my aunt is considered to be the family eccentric and is not to be taken seriously at all costs. However, I have once or twice thought that she knows more than she says. Why do you ask?"

Lucien pretended an interest in one lace cuff of his nightshirt. "Oh, no reason," he replied, plucking at a stray thread. "I was just making idle conversation, I suppose. Even now I dread being alone. It's silly of me, isn't it?"

"Perhaps I'll ask my aunt to sit with you this afternoon while I'm exercising my horse, Nemesis. Good day to you, Mr. Kendall, if I do not see you again today. I shall be very busy, you know, now that you are mending and not in such constant need of my services."

"I shall miss you, little one," Lucien breathed softly once Lady Penelope had closed the door behind her. "I believe I shall miss you quite a lot." Then he frowned, remembering how she had said his "past" would all come back to him. His past was Ann Louise, the real wife. Beautiful, cold, unfaithful Ann Louise. The thought of his wife brought the bitter taste of bile into his mouth, and he turned his mind to his unpleasant memories, hoping they would help to erase Lady Penelope's appealing image from his brain.

Lady Penelope's head was down as she left the room, and she nearly collided with her aunt in the hallway. Raising her eyes, she noticed the flush of color in Aunt Lucinda's cheeks, and correctly deduced that the woman had succumbed to listening at keyholes. "Why, Aunt," she teased, giving the woman a quick kiss, "what a happy coincidence that you should be here. I was just about to look for you. Our patient seems to have remembered his name. He is Lucas Kendall, of Surrey. He has a wife,

Annabel, and three small children. Isn't that above all things wonderful? That he should remember, that is. I'm so happy for him!''

Aunt Lucinda looked into her niece's suspiciously bright emerald eyes and gave a deep sigh. '' 'The lady doth protest too much, methinks,' Shakespeare,'' she pronounced sadly before moving off down the hallway toward her own chamber, leaving Lady Penelope behind to watch after her, stifling a sob with the back of one small hand.

Once inside her bedroom, Aunt Lucinda stood before her overloaded bookcase, reading the titles on the spines until she found the one that spelled out in gilt letters: *Miguel de Cervantes, His Works.* Reaching up to take the book down from the shelf, she then blew the light layer of dust off it and carried it with her to the desk that held her stationery.

She would write a letter. It was time she took a more active hand in things, before poor little Penelope's heart could be broken beyond repair. There was much plotting and mischief afoot, first on Lady Penelope's side, and now on Leighton's. Cervantes would be perfect for the task ahead of her, as his creation, Don Quixote de la Mancha, had much to say about the folly to be found in outlandish schemes.

Dipping her pen into the ornate, peacock-shaped well at the head of the desk, she drew out a crisp piece of paper and began to write, staying doggedly at her task for over two hours, making many references to the book that lay at her elbow as she frowned over her work.

The end result, although comprehensible to her, was sure to strike terror into the heart of the Marquess of Weybridge, who would receive the missive in a week's time. After rereading the letter a last time, Aunt Lucinda nodded her approval, sanded the page carelessly, then left it lying on the desk when the bell rang for luncheon.

The thin, spidery script, with grains of sand stuck to it in places and dotted here and there with blotches as the lady refused to take the time to repoint her pen, was left in the sunlight to dry. It read:

* * *

"I must speak the truth, and nothing but the truth." "Honesty's the best policy." "Forewarned forearmed." "By a small sample we may judge the whole piece."

"He's a muddled fool, full of lucid intervals." "More knave than fool." "He casts a sheep's eye at the wench."

"That's the nature of women . . . not to love when we love them, and to love when we love them not."

"Love and War are the same thing, and stratagems and policy are as allowable in the one as in the other."

"Those who'll play with cats must expect to be scratched." "Raise a hue and cry!" "Here's the devil-and-all-to-pay." "I begin to smell a rat."

" . . . a word to the wise is enough."

Chapter Eight

IT HADN'T precisely been the *worst* day in Lady Penelope's eventful young life, but it certainly ranked near the head of her list, right up alongside the day she had thrown a book at her brother Philippos in pique and ended up by shattering her father's favorite, hollow-eyed bust of Achilles all over the marble foyer floor (proving that more than the warrior's heel was vulnerable to assault as well as learning that, at the age of ten, she was not too old to be spanked), and it ranked even a few notches higher than the muggy summer afternoon she had decided to hide herself from Cosmo and Cyril in the caretaker's storage shed, and the silly man had locked her up with his axes and ladders (and a large family of inquisitive mice) by mistake.

This particular unhappy day, after riding Nemesis up and down the dreary countryside for several hours—leaving the unhappy Benedict groom two full fields behind her to grumble about the uselessness of trying to keep up with a she-devil on horseback while saddled with the broken-in-the-wind slug he had been forced to ride—she had hidden out in the garden, pretending an interest in the fading, rotting vegetation and the old gardener's rambling explanation of the proper way to mulch roses for the coming winter.

All the while, her beleaguered mind was crowded with the unhappy knowledge that her patient, Lucas Kendall, was a married man. Lucas Kendall, the man of the dark, laughing eyes and midnight black hair; Lucas Kendall, the man of the long, lean, muscled body and infuriating way of smiling at her as if he held the answer to all the secrets she had ever tried to unlock, had a wife tucked away in Surrey.

Lady Penelope's independent young spirit, her previously cheerful, buoyant demeanor, had been reduced to a sad, soggy mass, chock-full of conflicting emotions.

She hated him; she was intrigued by him.

She wanted him out of her life; she longed only to see him again.

She was glad he had remembered who he was; she wished he could have stayed anonymous forever.

Poor, confused, Lady Penelope had spent three days almost exclusively in his company, catering to his every whim, cooling his fevered brow, listening to his intelligent banter, learning to detect his slightest hint of discomfort. She had thought him a nuisance, had complained long and loud about his constant demands for attention, while all the time she had been blindly stumbling more and more deeply into the web of attraction he—like a cunning, clever spider—had been covertly spinning around her heart.

It was impossible. She had never yet met the man to scale her defenses. Yet she knew she could have escaped his embrace the day before if she had really wished it; could have given him a quick conk on the noggin and avoided the kiss that had shattered her mind, exploded all her hard-held beliefs, and turned her lifelong resolve to be independent of men into a pitiful, quivering tower of blancmange.

But he was married. She stood in front of a straggly rose bush, absently shredding the remnants of the last bloom of summer, still trying to assimilate the unbelievable—Lucas Kendall was married. He didn't seem like any married man of her acquaintance. He certainly didn't *act* like one, or hadn't until he had regained his memory and started waxing poetic about his worried wife—and his three children.

She pulled a face in the darkness. Sedgwick! Lord, what an uninspiring name. Such a wretched thing to do to an infant. Annabel must have had the naming of him, poor little baby. Anyone with a name like Annabel couldn't be trusted to know that Sedgwick was a totally unacceptable name.

She, Lady Penelope Rayburn, would never do anthing

so silly. Look how poor Philippos, Cyril, and Cosmo had suffered, thanks to the Marquess's love of Ancient Greece.

Of course, lugging the name Penelope about with her wasn't exactly an experience in unremitting joy either, she remembered with a grimace, recalling the way she had been teased by her playmates, who had pushed her to tears by calling out "Pe-nel-o-*pee,* Pe-nel-o-*pee,*" until she begged Philippos to teach her a few of the rudiments of pugilism and had then thoroughly thrashed Mary Louise Fletchley in front of the entire shocked congregation one day after church.

A reluctant smile lit her wan features for a moment as she thought of the way her father had roundly chastised her in public—after pulling her off Mary Louise's plump, nine-year-old stomach—only to reward her privately with a new pony for her fine "cross and jostle work." Perhaps Sedgwick would learn to be handy with his fives. Lucas could teach him.

Lucas.

The abused petals floated gratefully down to the relative safety of the damp ground as Lady Penelope shook her head and sighed. She had better go up and say good night to him. It wouldn't do to have him thinking she was avoiding him. Besides, he was probably as embarrassed about their intimate exchange of the day before as she was—even more so, actually, since he was the one with a wife.

She'd just go running upstairs and pop her head into the room for a minute to ask him how he felt tonight. After all, her guilty conscience reminded her, she'd been his nurse for three full days, and it would seem very strange if she deserted him now, just as he was beginning to recover so nicely.

Her decision made, Lady Penelope walked purposefully through the opened doors that led into the drawing room, only to be halted in her tracks by her Aunt Lucinda, who had been spending some time visiting with her late husband's homely Sheraton chairs.

" 'A penny for your thought,' Heywood," the older woman piped up cheerfully, for she had seen her letter to the Marquess leave with the post and was feeling quite pleased with herself at the moment. Banish her to the boredom of the country, would they? A lot her relatives knew—this was the most fun she'd had since that truly outstanding night last spring when she and the Dowager Duchess had successfully drunk each other under the table in the Duke's private study.

But it wouldn't do now to relax her vigilance. She wanted to be sure to keep herself up to date on Lady Penelope's activities. After all, the Marquess had warned her that the dear child was capable of almost anything.

"A halfpenny would be more than sufficient, Aunt," Lady Penelope assured her now, lowering herself gingerly onto the griffin-headed chair. "I was just on my way upstairs to check on Mr. Kendall. I've been, er, I've been very taken up with other things today and haven't visited with him since his good news this morning. Did you spend any time with him this afternoon? He told me how much he had enjoyed your short conversation after breakfast."

Aunt Lucinda shrugged modestly, although she was secretly pleased by the Earl's kind condescension. " 'I am but a gatherer and disposer of other men's stuff,' Wotton."

"Oh, Aunt, you're too modest," Lady Penelope protested. "I admit, I was rather confused by your rather *different* way of communicating when first I encountered it, but as time goes on I am beginning to see that you are really quite discerning. Indeed, I sometimes cannot help but feel that you know a great deal more than you tell. After all, you have been to London during the Season, haven't you, while I am nothing more than an ignorant provincial."

Busying herself with carefully wiping at the full, protruding bottom lip of one of the camel heads with the corner of her ornate lace handkerchief, Aunt Lucinda replied obliquely, " 'The fox knows many things, but the hedgehog knows one big thing,' Archilochus."

"See! There you go again!" Lady Penelope exclaimed, jumping to her feet. "How I wish, dear Aunt, that you came equipped with a guidebook, rather like the Elgin Marbles. I feel assured that such a handy reference would help me to better interpret and understand what you say. Ah, well, I imagine that we wouldn't be worthy of our title of Eve's daughters without our secrets, would we?"

Aunt Lucinda only smiled, then watched as her niece walked into the foyer to stand looking up the wide staircase. She could see the apprehension on Lady Penelope's small, upturned face and felt her heart go out to the girl.

Whatever game it was that the Earl of Leighton was playing with this farradiddle about being married, he'd better not dare to so much as harm a single hair on that lovely girl's head—or she, Lucinda Benedict, would make him wish he'd never been born. If she had learned nothing else during her short sojourn in London, she had vowed to emulate the example of dearest Tansy Tamerlane, now the Duke of Avonall's bride, who had never been backward in protecting the people in her charge.

She continued to watch as Lady Penelope put her hand out to catch at the newel post, bit her lip, sighed, and then slowly began dragging her reluctant feet up the carpeted staircase to face Lucien Kenrick—the man she thought of as Lucas Kendall; the man who had brought the proud young woman to the point of questioning her every movement.

Did the Earl of Leighton realize what a gem Lady Penelope was, what a rare prize he was perversely allowing to slip through his fingers? What was the matter with the man? Aunt Lucinda shook her head in confusion.

She had heard much about Leighton during her months spent chaperoning Lady Emily Benedict, and if she believed even half of it, he was the perfect match for Lady Penelope—bright, fun loving, and extremely personable—the most cherished guest of any hostess, unless she had a daughter of marriageable age, of course.

The man abhorred marriage; it was a commonly known fact, and one that did worry the matchmaking lady a little. But then, Aunt Lucinda thought bracingly, that was before he had met her niece. As she watched the hem of Lady Penelope's gown disappear up the staircase, she tilted her curly blonde head to one side and quoted softly, " 'She is the good man's paradise, and the bad's First step to heaven,' Shirley."

Lady Penelope may have been slightly comforted to know her aunt's high opinion of her (although she would have been much incensed to learn *all* that her aunt knew), and it may even have been enough to quell the tumultuous beating of her heart as her fingers closed around the cool, cut glass handle of the door to Lucien's chamber.

But she did not know, and she was left to face the man with her badly battered shield of feminine pride as her only armor. Taking a deep, steadying breath, she pasted a painfully bright smile on her face and rapped her knuckles softly against the wood paneling before pushing open the door and stepping inside.

The room was dark, with only one small brace of candles burning near the bedside, and the occupant of the bed seemed to be fast asleep.

Poor man, she thought sympathetically, he has been totally exhausted by the events of the day. After all, it is not every day that a man remembers he is a husband and father—and then has to find some way of dealing with the wild imaginings of an idiotic, adolescent girl he's had the bad judgment to punish with a kiss.

Lady Penelope was sure he knew that his kiss had affected her deeply; for he had shown concern in his carefully apologetic manner toward her that morning when he had told her about the existence of Annabel, saying, "My wife, yes. I'm—I'm so sorry."

She sighed yet again and made to leave the room, then stopped, a frown crossing her features. It was only just gone nine in the evening. Her patient had never settled down for the night before eleven, even when he was just beginning his recovery. Perhaps she'd better check on him, just to assure herself that he was all right.

So deciding (and before she could take the time to examine her motive more deeply to see if it had anything to do with her almost physical need to prolong the visit), she tiptoed across the room and bent down low over the bed in order to listen to the rhythm of his breathing.

He lay on his back, with his head resting on a single pillow, and his breathing seemed quite regular, if a bit deep, the faint rasp of a snore coming on every third breath. She reached out a hand and felt his cheek, searching for some sign of the slight fever that had plagued him for the first two days of his convalescence. He was cool to the touch, never moving as her fingers trailed along his jawline, then dared to draw themselves softly across his warm, slightly parted lips.

She leaned closer to admire the way his long, sooty lashes lay against his cheeks, her hand now resting on one broad, muscular shoulder. With her other hand, she lightly brushed back the unruly lock of hair that persisted in hanging over the bandage, feeling more courageous by the moment as he did not stir, but only seemed to smile in his sleep, as if her touch gave him pleasure.

"There you are, milady. Sleeping nice and peaceful-like, ain't he?"

Lady Penelope drew back her hands as if she had just encountered something hot and spun around to face the butler, who had crept into the room without a sound.

"Farnley! You—you startled me," she said quickly, wanting nothing more than to kick the nosy man out on his pointed ears. "I, um, I was checking on Mr. Kendall just now, before turning in myself. I think I, too, shall make it an early night. Let's hope Mr. Kendall doesn't have another cramp during the night to disturb us. We both could certainly use some rest. You, too, of course, Farnley, as you have, er, been invaluable, you know."

The butler advanced further into the room to stand at the bottom of the bed, a self-satisfied smile on his narrow face. "Oh, there'll be no problem with Mr. Kendall tonight, milady. I'd say the poppy petals did their job for us all right and tight, if you don't mind my saying so. We'll not be hearing nary a pip nor peep out of the poor gentleman before noontime tomorrow."

Lady Penelope looked inquiringly at the butler, then at Lucien (who was still dead to the world), and then back to the servant, who was now grinning like the village idiot. "Poppy petals, Farnley?" she asked, a niggling prickle of fear setting her pulse to racing. "Isn't that what they make opium from—and laudanum? You idiot man! Are you standing there telling me that you have *drugged* Mr. Kendall?"

Farnley raised his chin a fraction, highly insulted. "I didn't drug him, milady. I merely dosed him."

Her head shaking back and forth slowly, Lady Penelope could only gasp, "But—but, *why?* I don't understand."

94

"Mrs. Benedict was with him all afternoon," he told her, as if that explained everything.

"So? What does my aunt have to do with the thing, you daft creature? You may have killed him!" Lady Penelope had stopped looking at the butler, whom she longed to bash repeatedly about the head and shoulders with some appropriately lethal weapon, and was now concentrating on Lucien, shaking him gently by the shoulders in an effort to rouse him. When that didn't work, she gave him several sharp slaps on the cheek. He only moaned slightly and then rolled over onto his side, curling his head more deeply into the pillow.

Farnley sighed, knowing he had always been unappreciated. "Mr. Kendall had a blow to his head the other day, milady. With Mrs. Benedict in here all the day long, battering at his brainbox with her silly jabbering, there was no telling how he would be injured. The signs were all against his coming through such a threat to his recovery in one piece—I even heard an owl hooting at noon, and we all know what *that* means—so I took it upon myself to sprinkle some crumbled poppy flower into his rabbit stew tonight."

"I *still* don't understand," Lady Penelope exploded in exasperation. "Not that anything you could say now could possibly explain why Mr. Kendall has been treated so shamelessly. What good was there to be gotten from drugging the man?"

"That way we could be sure he at least got himself a good night's sleep," Farnley pressed on, wondering why he, such a learned man, had been forced to spend his life serving the uneducated. "Rest is the best protection against brain fever. Every child knows that. I haven't killed him, milady," he added scrupulously, "though, of course he did clean his plate real good. I should have taken into account that great appetite of his—quite a trencherman for an invalid Mr. Kendall is, isn't he, if you don't mind my saying so? Maybe he won't wake up until closer to dinnertime, milady. But he'll be right as a trivet then, you'll see."

Sinking down onto the edge of the high mattress, Lady Penelope whispered, "Oh, my Lord," and allowed her head to drop against her chest. "Farnley," she said softly, "I would suggest you take yourself out of here *now*, before I can muster up the strength to murder you." When the butler didn't move, she raised her head to look full into his face, her menacing expression making him wish he was daring enough to make the sign against the Evil Eye without ending up in even deeper trouble than it would appear he was in already.

"But, milady," he said hurriedly, "I haven't yet told you why I came upstairs hunting for you. There's two young gentlemen waiting downstairs to see you."

Farnley's words succeeded in gaining him Lady Penelope's attention. "Gentlemen? I wonder who they could be. I know no one in this area. Perhaps they've come to visit with my aunt, and you just misunderstood them."

The butler looked at her in exasperation. "I have two very good ears, milady," he corrected her, before qualifying that boast by adding that he sometimes wore spectacles now because his eyesight was "fading a tad for distance," thus insuring that no demons of physical misfortune would hear his claim to good health and meanly smite him down.

Lady Penelope nodded sympathetically and made a mental note to seek out the man's spectacles in the morning and hide them.

"They said they were your brothers," Farnley continued wearily. "Alike as peas in a pod they are, too, if you don't mind my saying so. Also, milady, it is a mite late for gentlemen callers to be dropping in on a female household, if you don't mind my saying so, seeing as how I am the only man around. Mrs. Benedict is probably already telling them so—not that they will have a chance of understanding her."

"Cosmo and Cyril are here?" Lady Penelope hopped to her feet, a bright smile replacing her frown. "I can't believe it!"

Farnley gave a toss of his head. "Well, I'm not lying, if that's what you mean, milady. There was a knock at the door, and when I opened it, there they were, big as life. Tossed their hats and canes at me like I was some underfootman—me, a man who was once valet to the Duke of

Avonall—and then they went waltzing off into the drawing room to meet Mrs. Benedict. That's when I came to fetch you. There's no telling what the old lady will say when she spies them out, if you don't mind my saying so."

Lady Penelope was torn between wishing to see her brothers and her reluctance to leave Lucien alone to sleep off his rare snootful of drugged rabbit stew. In the end, her longing to see Cosmo and Cyril overcame her fear—she truly could not believe Farnley had delivered a fatal dose of opium to the man—and she swept out of the room, ordering the butler to stay awake all the night long to watch over Mr. Kendall, or prepare to feel her wrath.

"And I warn you, Farnley—*if you don't mind my saying so*—I never want to hear you speak so disparagingly of Mrs. Benedict or my brothers again," she warned as she turned for one last worried look at her patient, "or else you will soon find yourself feeling lucky to be a second underfootman in Hades!"

Then she raced down the long flight of stairs as quickly as she could, calling out, "Cosmo? Cyril? Is it really you? Come here, you two rascals, and tell me how you ever managed to escape from Papa!"

Two identical dark blonde heads rapidly appeared around the corner of the open door leading to the drawing room, to be followed by two lean, fashionably attired male bodies. "Penny!" they called out happily in unison, nearly tumbling over each other as they ran to the bottom of the staircase to hold out their arms as their sister launched herself into the air, to land with an arm clasped around each of their necks, her feet dangling a good two feet above the floor as she showered kisses indiscriminately on the pair of them.

"Oh, you dear, dear darlings!" she exclaimed between kisses. "How I missed you rapscallions. Is Papa with you? *Please* say he is not. I have landed myself in the worst pickle, and he would absolutely *refuse* to understand that this time I am totally innocent."

"Penny, innocent?" Cosmo repeated questioningly, looking at his twin. "I say, Cyril, isn't that what the dean would call a contradiction in terms?"

"How should I know; you're the bookish one," Cyril

responded, disengaging himself from his sister's clinging arms. "Here now, Penny, leave off, do. You're creasing my new jacket. If we had known you'd react like this, we might not have come. All this hugging and kissing—it isn't fitting."

By this time Aunt Lucinda—who had been delighted to discover that the fashionable young gentlemen were related to Lady Penelope (and to herself, she remembered belatedly, making her joy that much greater)—had gathered herself together sufficiently to adjourn to a vantage point near the door to the drawing room and declared joyously, " 'Two of far nobler shape erect and tall, Godlike erect, with native honor clad in naked majesty seem'd lords of all,' Milton."

Cyril turned to look askance at his aunt, who had been spouting this same sort of nonsense at he and Cosmo for nearly ten minutes now, and tipped an imaginary hat in her direction, replying, "There once was a lass from Kilkenny, who'd do all you could ask for a penny. She—"

"Cyril!"

This combined outburst, coming as it did from both his brother and sister, effectively silenced the bawdy limerick, although Cyril was heard to mutter into his cravat, "Well, don't blame me. She's the one who said we was naked."

Cosmo started purposefully toward his brother, already beginning a lecture concerning just what could and could not be talked about in front of the ladies.

Lady Penelope quickly stepped forward to fill the breach, knowing that Cosmo, although he liked to pretend he was sophisticated, was not above tossing his brother to the floor and engaging in a friendly tussle to prove his point. "Aunt Lucinda!" she inserted loudly, walking over to slip her arm into the crook of Cosmo's elbow, restraining him. "Have my silly siblings introduced themselves to you? This is Cosmo, the elder, and Cyril is the one we usually keep on a leash. Isn't that right, Cyril, darling?"

Cyril scuffed the sole of one shiny Hessian against the tile floor. "Only once, Penny," he corrected sheepishly. "And I got you back for that, too."

It wasn't in Aunt Lucinda's nature to play favorites, but there was something about Cyril Rayburn that cut straight to her heart. She hurried over to tug on his arm, pulling him down so that she could plant a smacking kiss on one flaming red cheek, and then pronounced firmly, " 'A man he seems of cheerful yesterdays and confident tomorrows,' Wordsworth."

"Oh-ho, brother," Cosmo teased, winking broadly as he walked past his sibling to reenter the drawing room, "it would seem you've made a conquest. And you haven't been in the neighborhood above an hour. Never again will I say you're slow. You devil you!"

Lady Penelope hastened to follow after her brother, leaving Cyril to bring up the rear, with Aunt Lucinda still hanging coquettishly on his arm—not that the young man minded this attention for long, for he didn't, as the dear lady promptly directed him to the most comfortable chair in the room and then set a large brass bowl full of comfits on the table next to him before seating herself on a cushion at his feet. "You know what, ma'am," he said around a mouthful of the fruity confection, "I have decided that you are my favorite adopted aunt. You're my only adopted aunt, come to think of it, but I don't think you should hold that against me, do you?" He held out the bowl to her. "Comfit?"

Aunt Lucinda daintily dipped her fingers into the bowl and drew out one of the confections. Then, as Cyril made to pull the bowl away, she caught at his hand as she spied out one of her favorite nut-filled varieties and reached for another, saying, " 'Once more into the breach, dear friends, once more!' Shakespeare."

Cyril laughed, then leaned down to kiss his newfound aunt on the forehead. "We're going to be the best of good friends, Aunt, I promise you. Here, have another—I do believe this one is raspberry. Cosmo, Penny," he called out to his siblings across the room, "I think I'm in love!"

Seeing her aunt and brother Cyril enjoying themselves, and thankful to have Cosmo to herself for a moment, Lady Penelope quickly cornered him near Jerome Benedict's ugly legacies and pushed him unceremoniously into the one boasting the griffin heads before settling herself gingerly on the edge of the camel-head-backed chair. "Cosmo, I need your help," she said without ceremony.

"Yes, I rather gathered that," Cosmo replied, looking about him anxiously. "Penny, do these things bite? Very lifelike, ain't they?"

Lady Penelope reached out a hand to keep her brother from rising to his feet. "This house is crowded attic to cellar with all the stuff the Benedict family threw out of their other establishments. But you'd better not let Aunt Lucinda hear you speak jestingly about these chairs, or you'll break her heart. Her husband left these to her, you see. They're all she has of him now."

Cosmo pulled out his quizzing glass, stuck it to his eye, and examined the chairs at some length. "Didn't get on then, did they? Poor old thing. I don't remember when I've seen such a mass of ugliness—unless you consider Miss Abigail, of course. Oh, did I tell you? The spinster Pettibone has removed herself to St. Ives. Beautified the countryside no end, her leaving it. Didn't hurt old Archie Wilkinson much either. He has a gold tooth, did you know that? A lovely thing. You can see it very plainly now, as he's always smiling."

Lady Penelope resisted the urge to strangle her brother, whom she knew to be deliberately baiting her. Leaning back in her chair, she arched one dark eyebrow and said coolly, "If you've completely finished now? I am prepared to wait, however, if you have more interesting *bon mots* to impart. After all, I only have a drugged man lying upstairs in my chamber—a married man, no less, who thoroughly compromised me just yesterday afternoon. But that's only a piddling thing, isn't it, when compared with your news? Please, Cosmo, do go on. Tell me, has old Mrs. Masterson found her little doggy as yet? She was quite heartbroken when the ungrateful cur ran off just after that band of tinkers passed through the village."

Cosmo had bolted to his feet halfway through her blandly delivered monologue to look down at his sister, his mouth opening and closing rapidly as he looked for all the world like a beached fish. "You have a what—where? He did *what?* Good God, Penny, that's *not* funny."

Lady Penelope merely shrugged, "Oh, I admit it doesn't have all the hilarity of your little tale about the Pettibone, but then you must remember, I have been stuck away here at Wormhill for nearly a week. Nothing much happens in this area of the country during the latter half of the year.''

Cosmo collapsed back down onto the chair, heedless of the menacing griffins. ''Then you were just funning me? Don't do that, Penny. You nearly frightened me out of a year's growth. Now, seriously, what sort of trouble are you in this time that you don't want Papa within a hundred miles of this place?''

Lady Penelope took a deep breath and launched into her explanation. ''It happened the first day I was here, right after I realized the devious trick Papa had played on me by billeting me with Aunt Lucinda. You saw her, Cosmo. Papa knew I couldn't be kept out of mischief with that lovable nodcock as my keeper—he just *knew* it. Of course, I haven't done anything to the sweet, old dear, especially now that I've come to know her.''

''Well, I should certainly hope so,'' Cosmo interjected, looking over to where his aunt sat raptly listening to one of Cyril's sillier stories. ''She'd be so easy to fool that it would take all the sport out of the thing. So what did you do?''

''I took Nemesis out for a run—''

''Outrunning your groom in the process, of course,'' Cosmo cut in knowingly.

''Are you telling this story or am I?'' Lady Penelope challenged, sticking out her chin.

Cosmo reached out and tweaked her nose. ''You are, dearest sister. And you're not telling me a story, you're explaining how you were compromised by a drugged married man. Good Lord, we can just be thankful Papa isn't here!''

''I already said that,'' Lady Penelope reminded him, rubbing at her abused nose. ''Anyway, to continue, I was riding along, feeling much abused and uncharitable about all men, when out of the corner of my eye who should I spy but a gentleman, chasing me across the field.'' She closed her eyes as she remembered her first sight of Lucas Kendall. ''He was a really superb rider, and his mount was glorious—a huge black stallion that—''

''I'll hear all that later, if you please,'' Cosmo interrupted, beginning to worry. He didn't much like the look in his sister's eyes when she mentioned the rider of that stallion.

"Well then, to make a long story short, something you always say I cannot do, we somehow became engaged in a race. I thought *he* knew the jump was safe, and he must have thought that *I* did, though in reality we both did not, I suppose, or else neither of us would have attempted it, and he hit his head as he fell, losing his memory. I had him brought back here to Wormhill. He'd sprained his ankle as well, and had some terrible bruises on his ribs—"

"How do you know that?" Cosmo challenged, his eyes narrowing.

"Farnley told me," Lady Penelope replied, waving away his concern. "Anyway, he was badly injured, and it was all my fault. I should have known better than to race him, but it's just like Papa says, I set my mind on mischief and never think about the consequences. I decided then and there to mend my ways, and nurse the poor man back to health. That's why I was in the sickroom so much."

"Papa's been saying you were too wild for years, Penny. You never listened to him before; why did you have to pick now to become a dutiful daughter?"

"Well, it doesn't matter one way or the other anymore, does it, because Mr. Kendall has now regained his memory, and recalled that he is a married man and the father of three children. If only he had remembered that before he pulled me down on top of him in bed and kissed me, I think I could reconcile myself to—"

"He did what!"

Lady Penelope pressed a hand against Cosmo's mouth, silencing him. "Keep your voice down, you idiot. What if Aunt Lucinda should hear you? Besides, that's the least of my problems now, because Farnley—he's Aunt Lucinda's butler and the saddest, sorriest human being that ever lived—drugged poor Mr. Kendall tonight because—well never mind why, that isn't important either."

Cosmo dropped his forehead into his hands and sighed. He and Cyril had come to Wormhill because they had found life at Weybridge boring without their sister there to liven their days with her playfulness. Now he was wishing the both of them snugly back there, with nothing to do but wiggle their thumbs. "What *is* important, Penny? And, please, hurry with your explanation. I believe, like my father before me, that you are giving me the headache."

Lady Penelope leaned closer to her brother, her voice low as she said, "What is important *now*—since you and Cyril so obligingly showed up here in my hour of need and can help me accomplish it—is that Mr. Lucas Kendall must be removed from Wormhill as soon as possible and installed at some local inn until he is fit to continue his travels. He has to be moved tonight, while he's still drugged and won't know what's happening."

"Why? Why tonight? Besides, I think I should be calling the man out—once he's recovered, that is."

"Because I can't face him anymore, that's why," his sister admitted, tears stinging her eyes. "And you can't go calling him out. It isn't his fault that he kissed me. He didn't know he was married until this morning. The man is totally innocent and is only lying up there because of me. Besides, I have to get him out of the house before Papa can show up here—and he will, if you two have escaped Weybridge without his permission, which I can see by the look on your face is exactly what you have done—and sees for himself how I've botched everything again with my silly pranks. Otherwise I shall be forced to have that Season in London that was part of our wager. Please, Cosmo, you and Cyril *have* to help me. I don't know what else to do."

Cosmo searched his sister's face, seeing the tears and the hurt that were stamped so clearly on her features. "This Lucas Kendall didn't do anything, uh, you know . . . ?"

Lady Penelope bit her lip and shook her head. "He's totally innocent. I merely got what I deserved, Cosmo. Papa may not know it yet, but he has won far more from me than a silly wager. I vow to you—once I am safely out of this mess and back at Weybridge, I shall *never* play pranks again!"

Chapter Nine

LADY Penelope Rayburn's resolve to mend her prankish ways and be good was heartfelt.

It was, however—alas—also short-lived.

It lasted until Aunt Lucinda reluctantly rose from her cushion to head for her bed, lingering girlishly over her good nights to Cyril.

It persisted as Cosmo filled Cyril in on all that had happened to their dearest baby sister since they had waved the poor girl goodbye at Weybridge Manor, and while Cyril delivered a rather rambling homily on the wickedness to be found in the wilds of Derbyshire.

It even prevailed during their stealthy trip up the broad staircase and down the long hall to the door of her patient's bedchamber. It lasted, in fact, until she opened the door to that chamber, and Cyril exclaimed in shocked accents, "Good Lord, it's Lucien Kenrick!"

"*What?*" Lady Penelope squeaked, unprepared for this potentially damning information.

"Well, ain't it, Cosmo?" Cyril questioned, eager for assurance. "That's the Earl of Leighton Penny's got tucked up over there fast asleep, sure as check. You remember, don't you, Cosmo? We met him last year in London when we sneaked away from school to visit Philippos. What's Penny doing drugging Lucien Kenrick?" He turned to look at his sister. "Penny," he repeated, "what in blue blazes d'ya think you're doing—drugging an Earl?"

But his sister wasn't attending and hadn't been for some moments. She had heard the name Lucien Kenrick, and the blood had grown cold in her veins. Lucas Kendall. Lucien Kenrick. Her ears began to pound in rhythm with the agitated beat of her heart. Little Sedgwick's father. A lying, conniving son of a—*"I'll kill him!"*

"Now, Penny," Cosmo warned, pulling her back against his chest by the shoulders as Lady Penelope started forward, her hands squeezed into tight fists. "Just hold on a moment before you go off half-cocked. There has to be some reasonable explanation for all this."

"There is," she fumed from between clenched teeth as she struggled vainly to free herself from her brother's grasp. "The man's been running a rig ever since he got here! He never lost his memory—he was just playing on my sympathy. First he has me waiting on him hand and foot, then he steals a kiss as if I were some kind of—well, never mind that—and then he makes up that *ridiculous* farradiddle about being a married man with three children when he thinks his arrogance may have gotten him in too deep. Oh, the monster! I ought to choke him!"

"Penny, I think you're becoming hysterical," Cosmo interrupted. "Please calm yourself. I don't want to have to slap you or something."

But his sister had gotten the bit between her teeth and was not to be brought back under control so quickly. *"Sedgwick!* I should have known. How could I have been so stupid, so gullible? I'm going to kill him, Cosmo, so don't try to stop me. And when I'm finished with him, I'm going to find dearest Philippos and murder him, too. This prank has his mark stamped all over it! Now let me go!"

Cosmo coughed and sputtered, trying to get an errant lock of Lady Penelope's wildly flying hair out of his mouth. Still holding her tightly against his chest as her feet dangled inches off the floor, he urged, "Be reasonable—and stop kicking at my shins with your heels. It hurts. Killing the man won't solve anything, Penny. Think about it. There must be another way, something we could do that would even the score. He deserves killing, there's no doubt about that, but wouldn't it be even better if we could find some way to turn the tables on him, give him back a dose of his own medicine?"

Cyril, who wasn't sure he understood everything that was going on, but who recognized the chance for a bit of frolic when it presented itself, quickly added his approval, saying happily, "He's really out cold, ain't he, Cosmo? We could strip him down and hang him up in the middle of the square in that village we passed through a while back. What d'ya say, Penny? Sound good to you?"

Lady Penelope stopped struggling, her slight body sagging back against her brother as she gave herself over to thought, her head slowly tilting this way and that as she stared at the somnolent Lucien Kenrick, assessing her options. "He looks very peaceful, doesn't he, boys? He's survived his fall, recovered his memory—or so he says—and is well on his way to a full recovery. How absolutely terrible it would be for him now if he were to have a relapse."

"What are you thinking, Penny?" Cosmo questioned, relaxing his grip on her shoulders once he was assured she wasn't about to leap on top of the drugged man and pummel him into splinters. "Not that I like Cyril's idea overmuch, you understand, but I don't think I like that tone in your voice. It's bad enough the man's been drugged, I won't be a party to poison."

"I said 'relapse,' Cosmo. Poison has nothing to do with it. Now be quiet, I have to think."

Cyril, who was beginning to feel the effects of his overindulgence into the tasty comfits Aunt Lucinda had been pushing on him all evening long, tottered over to the chair on the window side of the bed and gratefully sank into it. He looked at Lucien assessingly. "You sure he ain't toes up already, Penny? He's awfully still."

"His lordship is perfectly well, if you don't mind my saying so," came a thin, reedy voice from the shadows, causing Cyril to bounce back to his feet in alarm. "I am always extremely careful with my portions."

"Farnley!" Lady Penelope exclaimed, exasperated to learn that she and her brothers had been overheard. "What do you think you're doing here?"

The butler gingerly stepped out from the dark corner he had been standing in (being very careful not to cough and thereby disclose his presence before he had heard everything of importance) and bowed his head slightly in Lady Penelope's direction. "You told me to stay with his lordship all the night long, milady, if you don't mind my reminding you. It's not my place to say this, but I should like to assist you in your plans, if I may. His lordship has all but run me ragged—and my dearest Pansy, too—with his nonsense.''

Lady Penelope smiled, biting her bottom lip as she surveyed her three cohorts in unladylike glee, her emerald eyes sparkling in the dim candlelight. It could work. If they all played their parts correctly, it just could work.

''Yes-s-s,'' she said at last, dragging out the word evilly, before tossing her head so that her tangled curls arranged themselves around her shoulders like a red-gold mantle, giving her the appearance of a naughty angel. ''I think I should like that, Farnley, my friend. I think I should like that above all things. Gentlemen?'' she prompted lightheartedly, motioning toward the door to the hallway. ''May I suggest that we adjourn to the drawing room now, to discuss strategy?''

Cyril playfully nudged his brother in the ribs as they followed Lady Penelope down the broad staircase. ''Here we go again, brother. Ain't it grand?''

There was a dry, cottony taste in his mouth, and his tongue felt twice its size as it tried in vain to find a comfortable spot to lie behind his aching teeth. Moving his head slightly on the pillow, he felt the heavy—and almost familiar—dull thump-thumping that told him better than anything else that he had somehow gotten himself a rare, crushing bruiser of a hangover.

He couldn't remember anything of the happenings of the previous evening, but he hoped he had enjoyed himself, for he certainly was going to pay for it this morning—in spades. He groaned self-pityingly as his stomach performed a nasty little flip, as if considering whether or not it really wished to continue offering refuge to its contents.

''*He's awake!* Isn't it above everything *wonderful?* Oh, Doctor Fell, come here quickly and see for yourself! And you said it wouldn't happen. Well, I just knew it, really I did. I never gave up hope. *Mr. Kendall is finally awake!*''

Lucien heard Lady Penelope's voice from somewhere above his head and struggled to open his eyes. The effort was beyond him, and he stuck out the tip of his tongue to moisten his parched lips, trying to form one of the many questions he longed to ask.

So I'm awake—why make such a fuss about it? I awake every morning; it is quite a natural occurrence. Why is she carrying on like some missish hysteric? Who in blazes is this Doctor Fell person she's screaming at anyway? And why can't I open my damned eyes?

"Yes, yes, of course, Lady Penelope," he heard a man's voice saying pettishly. "Mr. Kendall does, indeed, seem to be coming awake at long last. It's a very promising sign, I admit, although you realize it does not guarantee he will live. I had begun to despair for him, you know, and I still have my reservations."

I do not love thee, Doctor Fell, Lucien found himself silently quoting the first line of Tom Brown's facetious poem as he felt the doctor's cold hands examining his nude body under the coverlet. What had happened to his nightshirt? he wondered, thankful that he could feel the coverlet against his shoulders. After all, Lady Penelope was in the room.

"I know, Doctor. I remember everything you've told me since Mr. Kendall suffered this terrible relapse. It has been three days since our butler, Farnley, found him lying here unconscious." Lady Penelope's voice was soft, scarcely above a whisper, and Lucien swallowed down hard, realizing she was talking about him.

Three days? I've been lying here for three days? Unconscious?

"Such a development is not unusual in such cases, my lady, as head injuries are the very Dev—I mean, head injuries can be quite peculiar," he heard the doctor reply in what Lucien could only think of as a supercilious tone. "But I would have been ignoring my sacred oath if I had not told you not to get your hopes up for a recovery. This could still be only a temporary rally."

The reason why I cannot tell, his confused brain continued the recitation, rambling on: But this alone I know full well—

"One can only hope he shall not need to be bled again,"

continued the physician. "Such a nuisance. My supply of leeches runs low."

I do not love thee, Doctor Fell. Leeches! Leighton's body jerked almost completely into the air as he struggled against the thought of those fat, ugly creatures sucking at his skin.

"What—what in bloody *hell* is going on here?" he exploded, struggling to rise. He tried once more to open his eyes, but his bandage must have slipped, because he could now feel the cloth that prevented him from seeing Lady Penelope and the pessimistic Doctor Fell.

Well, he'd soon remedy that—among other things! He made to lift his right hand from the mattress, only to find that it moved no more than a foot before being stopped by cloth bindings which held him firmly tied to the bed at the wrist. He jerked angrily on the restraint, but to no avail, then tried to move his left hand.

It was no use. He was well and truly locked against the mattress. Even his ankles were similarly shackled. He felt like Gulliver in the land of the Lilliputians. "Lady Penelope!" he called out fretfully, twisting his head from side to side as he tried blindly to search out her direction. "What's happening? Why am I tied down? Remove this damned—*dratted* bandage at once!"

He felt Lady Penelope's cool hand on his cheek and relaxed a little, giving a heartfelt sigh. She was here; he hadn't been imagining things. Sane heads would rule at last. Stupid, old woman doctor! Lady Penelope wouldn't let him down. "Thank God, Lady Penelope. For a minute there I thought I'd been transported overnight to Lilliput, and Doctor Fell was the Emperor. Please, uncover my eyes for me and tell me what this foolishness is all about."

"Lilliput? Oh, dear, I think he must be delirious, Doctor," he heard Lady Penelope say, her voice thick with what Lucien assumed were unshed tears, just before her comforting hand trailed slowly away, and he was left all alone once more. "I can see now why you insisted he be put in restraints. His brain fever has made him quite strong, and he might injure himself. Poor, poor, Mr. Kendall. I've sent off a note by messenger to his wife in Surrey, of course, We can only hope she and the children arrive in time.''

"In time for what, you silly woman?" Lucien bellowed angrily, although his heart was beginning to pound. Had the whole world run mad? "I'm not sick. I'm *never* sick. This is ridiculous. Untie me at once, do you hear!''

"Shush now, Mr. Kendall, you must save your strength. Little—little Sedgwick will be with you shortly," he heard Lady Penelope say comfortingly, her voice cracking with emotion, before the faint clicking of her heels against the wooden floor beside the bed told him she was leaving—leaving him alone and defenseless with only Doctor Fell and his bloody leeches for company.

"Lady Penelope!" he called after her, fighting the restraints on his wrists like a wild animal caught in a trap. "Don't leave me like this, I beg you. I'm sorry I yelled at you, really I am. Stay with me, dear Lady Penelope. I—I'm not a well man.''

His only answer came in the soft closing of the door, and he braced his body against the onslaught he was sure would come. He was alone in the chamber with the sadistic Doctor Fell and his thirsty leeches. Lady Penelope had gone, deserted him in his hour of need, and if he were not a grown man, he would like nothing more than to break down and wail.

"Don't you touch me, you charlatan," he warned Doctor Fell loudly, "or else once I am up from this bed I shall cut your miserable heart out and feed it to you for good measure. Do you hear me, you miserable leech? Answer me, damn you! *Answer me!*''

Lucien held his breath for a long time, listening to the silence that filled the room. They were gone, he realized at last, sighing with relief. They were both gone, leaving him sick, maybe even dying, and utterly alone.

What Leighton did not, could not, know was that Lady Penelope and her brother Cosmo—who had done such a superior job in his role as the morbid Doctor Fell—had no choice but to leave the Earl alone.

After all, it would have thoroughly destroyed their plan if they had lingered too long and he had heard their delighted laughter!

"He thought he was Gulliver? That's rich, 'pon my soul, it is!" Cyril crowed, leaning against his brother in his glee. "I don't know how you kept a straight face through it all. Doctor Fell, indeed. Couldn't you think of a better name than that old biscuit?" he asked before he and Cosmo threw back their heads and laughed aloud.

" 'All who joy would win must share it—happiness was born a twin,' Byron," Aunt Lucinda trilled from the sidelines, enjoying their obvious delight. She and Cyril had been waiting in the drawing room all the day long, until the Earl had finally shown signs of wakening just before dinner.

The older woman had been pleased to have been made the confidante of the little group, not bothering to tell them that she had known Leighton's true identity from the beginning, but only refraining from trying to talk them out of their little revenge. She would call a halt to the scheme if it went on too long, but for now she was content to join in the fun.

Lady Penelope, who had just come downstairs after changing her gown for dinner, entered the room and joined her aunt on the settee, settling her pale blue silk skirts around her demurely. "Like little children who have escaped their governess, aren't they, Aunt?" she remarked placidly, just as if she herself hadn't been in her room, dissolved in giggles with Doreen over the whole affair not an hour earlier. "It takes so little to amuse some people. Did I hear Farnley say Pansy was preparing a special treat for us this evening? Anyone would think we have something to celebrate."

Aunt Lucinda turned to look at her niece, who was sitting beside her so demurely, as if butter wouldn't melt in her mouth, and voiced her appreciation of the girl's genius. " 'Her wit was more than man, her innocence a child,' Dryden," she quoted, patting Lady Penelope's modestly folded hands.

"Dinner is served," Farnley announced in stentorian tones from the doorway, bowing in a way that told them better than words that he considered himself to be the only responsible person among them.

" 'A beetle-headed, flat-ear'd knave,' Shakespeare," his mistress grumbled, struggling to her feet amid her yards and yards of pink tulle skirt. Then, patting at her dyed blonde curls, which had been piled high on her head in celebration of some secret triumph she was not about to share with her young relatives, she took Cyril's proffered arm and led the way into the small dining room.

It wasn't until later, after they had finished polishing off Pansy's major triumph—a delicious, Madeira-flavored syllabub—that Cyril began having second thoughts about what they were doing to the Earl of Leighton. "Seems a bit much, you know," he said, licking the last of the creamy dessert from the back of his spoon. "I mean, we're keeping the man a prisoner, if you get right down to it. Have we even fed him?"

Laying her hand affectionately on his sleeve, Aunt Lucinda batted her scanty eyelashes and purred, " 'A certain Samaritan . . . had compassion on him,' Luke, 10:33."

"Oh, well now, Auntie," Cyril protested, coloring hotly as his brother and sister stuffed their serviettes into their mouths to keep from laughing out loud, "I wouldn't go so far as to call me a *Samaritan,* would you Cosmo? It's not that I think we should let the fellow off scot-free. He did pull a very nasty trick on our sister here, didn't he? I just think we should draw the line at starving the man to death."

Lady Penelope, still wiping tears of mirth from her eyes at the sight of Cyril's obvious discomfiture, assured her brother that starving the Earl was the furthest thing from her mind. "Farnley is upstairs with him now, feeding him some lovely invalid gruel by hand. I realized that our patient's diet has been particularly heavy—full of roasted meat and such—and decided that it would be better for his poor, relapsed constitution if he were reduced to weak broth and watered milk for a few days. That is standard practice for invalids. After all, Cyril, I am his nurse." Turning to Cosmo with a wink, she ended, "Isn't that right, Doctor Fell?"

" 'The Devil can quote scripture for his purpose,' Shakespeare," Aunt Lucinda reminded Lady Penelope, although her voice held no sting of reproach.

"Yes, but—"

"Oh, leave off, brother," Cosmo said imperatively, rising to his feet. "The man compromised our sister, it's as plain as glass. If she wants us to help her get a little of her own back, who are we to question her? After Penny's had her measure of fun with him, we'll summon Papa—if he isn't already on his way, on the hunt for us—and the two of them will be married. It's as simple as that."

"*Married!*" Lady Penelope screeched—for, daughter of a Marquess or nay, the shrill piercing sound could only have been so described—and jumped to her feet, knocking over her chair, which loudly crashed against the parquet floor. "Cosmo, have you lost your mind? I'm never going to marry, you already know that. And I'm *certainly* not about to wed that miserable, two-faced, lying libertine upstairs. I'd sooner drown myself in the Thames!"

"I doubt Papa would allow that," Cosmo supplied calmly, bending down to right the toppled chair. He'd given the subject a lot of thought the night before while he and Cyril had stripped the Earl down to the buff and trussed him up like a Christmas goose, and he'd come to realize that, as both his Papa and Philippos were unavailable, it was up to him to make sure justice was served and the honor of his sister protected. Marriage was the only sensible answer, even if he had to literally truss both the bride and groom up in knots to accomplish the deed.

Oh, there was another way to satisfy the Rayburn honor, but Cosmo had dismissed that idea as soon as it had entered his head. The Earl of Leighton was a tall, muscular creature, and years ahead of him in experience; certainly no fair match either with his fists or a weapon. No, a duel was out of the question, and the alternative—delivering him a sound whipping—was even more ludicrous. After all, they couldn't keep the man tied up forever. He was bound to get loose sooner or later, and then there'd be the devil to pay.

Yes, Cosmo had thought of everything, and marriage was the only remedy. He looked across the table to where his Aunt Lucinda was sitting, a bright smile on her face, and realized that he had just stepped up a notch in her estimation. Not adverse to gathering all the reinforcements about him that he could, he bowed encouragingly in her direction and asked her opinion on the subject.

" 'Domestic happiness, thou only bliss of paradise that has survived the fall,' Cowper," the lady pronounced, clasping her hands together across her bosom. She had rather hoped dearest Cyril would have thought of something so obvious, but as long as the desired result was to be gained, she imagined it didn't really matter much either way exactly who was the author of the deed. Her elaborate coiffure hadn't been in vain. There would be a celebration!

Lady Penelope looked to her brother Cyril, who was busily pushing together the crude design of a church out of cookie crumbs on the tablecloth, then to Cosmo, who was looking more like Papa than she would have liked, and lastly, at Aunt Lucinda, who only tilted her ridiculously curled head at her benignly and smiled.

"You think all you have to do is say it, and it will happen? That I have nothing to say in the matter? And I thought you loved me!" she wailed, bursting into tears.

"Well, I won't have it!" Lady Penelope declared, already running from the room. "I won't have any of it, do you hear me?"

"I think they heard her in Bond Street," Cyril remarked, rubbing his abused ears. "The sound really bounces off the walls in these closed rooms, don't it? What do you think she'll do now, Cosmo? I wouldn't put it past her to murder the Earl, just to get out of marrying him."

"I can't worry about that now, Cyril," his brother replied, his gaze still on the opened doorway Lady Penelope had passed through just a few moments earlier, in high dudgeon. "It's her eventual revenge on *us* that truly terrifies me."

"Please, sir, open your mouth," Farnley begged wearily, holding out the spoonful of barley broth. "There's only a few bites left, and then I can give you the rest of your nice warm milk."

"I'll give you—"

Lucien's angry words, meant to inform the butler of just what the Earl would like to give him and how, were effectively cut off as Farnley quickly shoveled the spoon into his open mouth. "That's the ticket, sir. You need to keep up your strength. That necklace of red coral I hung 'round your neck after Doctor Fell left is still pale, proving to me that you're still a very sick man, no matter how much better you feel. Drink up all your milk now, and maybe by dawn tomorrow we'll see a little of its color coming back."

"You'll see *color*, all right, and long before morning, you idiot twit," Lucien snapped irritably, for he had been lying in this very uncomfortable position for over six hours and had long since lost any patience he might have had. "These damned rocks are so sharp they should be covered with my life's blood before another hour is out. Now stop pushing that cup at me and listen. I haven't suffered a relapse, it's all a hum. I'm being kept a prisoner here against my will. I need your help. Cut me loose, and you'll be a rich man, Farnley, I promise you."

"Oh, is it rich you're goin' to be now, Farnley?" Doreen Sweeney asked from the doorway. She had thought it wise to keep an eye on the butler, no matter how he had managed to hoodwink her mistress into believing he was one of them. Farnley was about as loyal as a hungry dog at its master's wake. Well, she, Doreen Fiona Elizabeth Sweeney, would soon put an end to this! "It's true then," she mused, hands on hips, "the Devil is good to his own. Tell me now, greedy guts, what is it you'll be doin'? Are you so hot for gold that you'd listen to the ravin's of a sick man?"

Recognizing the maid's booming Irish brogue, Lucien tried yet again to sit up, straining mightily against his bonds. "It's true, blast you, woman," he cried out angrily. "I'm not delirious. I'm Lucien Kenrick, Earl of Leighton, and I can make Farnley rich. I can make *both* of you rich. Just untie these knots for me, and I can prove it."

Doreen winked conspiratorially in Farnley's direction as she approached the foot of the bed. "Is it after making a fool of me you'd be, Mr. Kendall?" she asked, enjoying herself. "I can see you tryin' it with Farnley here. That googeen heard the money jinglin' in his mother's pockets before he was born. He'd believe anything, if he was to profit from it, don't you know. But you won't be foolin' me with your tall tales. Lady Penelope checked all through your belongin's when first you got here, and there ain't stitch nor seam that says anythin' to the point about you. An Earl, is it? Sure you are, and I'm Queen of the May! It's sick you are, and no mistake. Now why don't you just rest easy, Mr. Kendall, and let Farnley here tend you?''

Lucien collapsed against the mattress in defeat. Either the servants truly believed he was delirious, or they were in on the deception like everyone else. Doctor Fell, indeed! It may have taken him a little while to figure it all out, but the truth of the situation had finally dawned on him. They were playing him for a fool, all of them!

Somehow—although the details of that part of the thing he had not as yet figured out—they had discovered his true identity, and now he was being made to pay the piper. Lady Penelope may be many things, but she was not a consummate actress. Her heavy-handed grief over ''little Sedgwick'' had all but given the game away—once he had calmed enough to think things through, that is. Now she was out for revenge, and she had certainly not held herself to any half measures. Philip would be proud of her.

Philip! Was he Doctor Fell? That would go a long way toward explaining what's happening to me now, Lucien thought. Philip must certainly think he owes me something for tucking him into bed with that salmon.

Lucien tried with all his might to remember the exact tone of the man who had been speaking of leeches and certain death that afternoon. No, he decided at last, it couldn't have been Philip. The voice wasn't deep enough. Damn this blindfold! He'd spent over an hour that afternoon rubbing his head against the edge of the pillow, nearly dislodging the cloth, before Farnley had come in to feed him and retied the bandage even tighter than before.

''Listen to me,'' he pushed on now, trying hard to keep his voice low and his temper under control. ''Whether you believe me or nay, I *am* the Earl of Leighton. I was drugged, I'm sure of it, and then tied up like this. Your mistress is keeping me prisoner here against my will, and you're helping her. When I am finally freed—as I assure you I will be—it would go better for you if I could tell the authorities that you two helped me. Prison is a dark, cold place, you know.''

Doreen merely sniffed. "It's quiverin' in m'boots you have me, Mr. Kendall, don't you know. His brains are surely scrambled. When it comes to tellin' tales, he sure beats Banaghan, don't he, Farnley? Farnley?''

The butler didn't answer, but just stood beside the bed, thoughtfully worrying his bottom lip. Prison? He didn't want to go to prison. Fun was fun, and it wasn't as if the Earl didn't deserve it, but the butler hadn't thought about prison. How would Pansy ever go on without him around to guide her? And then there was that nonsense about being drugged. Farnley knew he had only dosed the man for his own good, but who'd believe the word of a butler over that of an Earl? "I—I don't know," he stammered. "Perhaps we should—"

"Blast your black soul, Farnley, for only thinkin' of your own neck!" Doreen advanced toward the butler, whom she outweighed by two stone, her fist in the air.

"No, no! I didn't mean it, truly I didn't," Farnley whined, as he was very easily cowed. Prison might lie in his future, but Doreen Sweeney was hovering menacingly in his present. He stepped back a pace, assuring her fervently, "I won't let him go. I swear it on my dear mother's head."

"Better for you to go down on your two bended knees and give thanks to God that I don't tell Lady Penelope what a snivelin', two-faced ferret you are," Doreen warned him before turning on her heels and stomping toward the doorway to check on her mistress who had come up to her chamber a few minutes earlier in quite a state. As there seemed to be nothing amiss in the sickroom, she'd have to go back to Lady Penelope and see what had happened to put her in such a flutter. "It's back here tomorrow mornin' at first light I'll be, Farnley, and it will go bad for you if Mr. Kendall isn't lyin' here sloppin' up some more of your gruel, and no mistake."

Hearing the door close, Lucien whispered bracingly, "You're not afraid of her, are you, my friend? She can't do anything to you, you know. Now be a good fellow and cut me loose. I can understand why I'm being treated like this, but I think I've been punished enough, don't you? We men must stick together, right, Farnley?''

The butler reached up one hand and eased the sudden tightness that had invaded his throat. He had never had any of these problems when he was valet for the Duke— except maybe that time Miss Tamerlane took him along to stop that duel—and for a moment he wished himself back in London and out of this madness. "I don't know what you're talking about, Mr. Kendall,'' he said at last, his thin voice squeaking like an unoiled gate as he made himself busy with the dinner tray. "You're a sick man, you know, sir, and me, why, I'm only following Lady Penelope's orders. Now, please let me raise your head so that you can drink down this milk. There's only a little skin on it.''

Lucien Kenrick, knowing when he was beaten, drank the milk.

Farnley finally departed, leaving Lucien alone in the room with only his anger and his conscience for company. After running off a lengthy string of colorful curses that would have had even his friend Philip covering his ears, the Earl tried to tell himself that things would be better in the morning.

Lady Penelope had had her little revenge now—and a brilliant revenge at that, for, at least for a while, he had truly believed he was ill—but she wasn't really the vindictive sort. She'd probably demand an apology from him, then order his bonds cut and his clothing returned to him. After all, what he had done wasn't all that terrible. So he'd lied about his identity; there was no real harm in that.

You kissed her, his conscience jabbed at him, rudely reminding the Earl of something he wanted to forget. You pulled her down onto the bed and kissed that gorgeous creature senseless—not Lucas Kendall, but you, the Earl of Leighton. The unmarried Earl of Leighton. You ran your licentious hands over her lush young body, enjoying every wonderful, decadent moment of it, thoroughly compromising an innocent girl. Then you cravenly tried to weasel your way out of taking responsibility for your actions by claiming you were a married man. You deserve

118

all the punishment she can hand out. Hanging's too good for you!

Lucien closed his lips into a tight, thin line, knowing that his conscience was right. If he were any kind of a gentleman, he would have immediately owned up to what he'd done and offered to marry the girl. In fact, he realized with a jolt, that was probably what this whole thing was about—he was being held captive until the Marquess showed up, breathing fire, and with a cleric in tow.

"Penelope wouldn't do that to me," he said out loud, remembering his jailer's feelings toward the wedded state while not realizing that he had neglected to refer to her as *Lady* Penelope. "She's as opposed to marriage as I am. No, I don't believe I have to worry about the Marquess. She's just giving me a lesson in humility for deceiving her, for running her ragged doing my bidding. She'll be in here first thing tomorrow morning to release me. We'll both have a good laugh and then forget the whole thing. She's a good sport; she must see the humor in it. She isn't missish."

Turning his head to one side, Lucien tried to concentrate on going to sleep. Everything would be straightened out in the morning, and by noon he would be on his way to Scotland, his strange interlude in Wormhill—and his association with one Lady Penelope Rayburn—safely behind him.

The thought failed to bring a smile to his lips.

Chapter Ten

LUCIEN awoke all at once, instantly aware that someone else was in the room with him. Whether or not the long night was finally over and it was morning, he could not tell, for the bandage over his eyes was still, maddeningly, in place. Struggling to keep his breathing even, he continued to feign sleep, wondering who was standing beside his bed and what was going to happen next. By this time, he had learned to expect anything.

His visitor must have realized he was awake, for suddenly he felt a hand creeping behind the pillow, raising his head to the cup that banged sharply against his front teeth. He drank the hot, sweet liquid gratefully, for the warm milk that idiot Farnley had forced down his throat the night before had left a terrible, cloying taste on the roof of his mouth that had been plaguing him mercilessly ever since.

" 'Tea! thou soft, thou sober sage, and venerable liquid;—thou female tongue-running, smile-smoothing, heart-opening, wink-tippling cordial, to whose glorious insipidity I owe the happiest moments of my life, let me fall prostrate!' Cibber," he heard Lucinda Benedict trill above him in her high, childish voice.

"You quote Colley Cibber, madam?" Lucien asked after draining the cup, deciding to move more slowly with this potential rescuer. After all, he couldn't really offer her a bribe, as he had Farnley and Doreen. This time he would use finesse rather than threats and bluster. "I should think you'd shun him, as his mutilation of Shakespeare's work is so well known. But perhaps you, like me, applaud him for his many fine plays. I was fortunate enough to attend a presentation of his *Love's Last Shift, or the Fool in Fashion* in London last year, and have read his biography. Truly, the man was born before his time. He would have been right at home sparring with Sheridan.'' Then, thinking he had paved the way sufficiently with this nonsense, he went on brightly, ''Please, ma'am, would you tell me the time?''

He could hear the soft rustling of Mrs. Benedict's skirts as she walked around the bottom edge of the bed and settled herself into the straight-backed chair near the window. '' 'I never knew the old gentleman with the scythe and hour-glass bring anything but grey hairs, thin cheeks, and loss of teeth,' Dryden,'' she quoted obliquely, just as the clock in the hallway helpfully chimed out the hour of seven, giving him an answer that was definitely more to the point.

''So it *is* morning,'' Lucien said, turning his bandaged head in the general direction of the window, knowing the sun should be warming his face shortly, if, indeed, it was not raining. ''I wonder, Aunt Lucinda—and please forgive my familiarity, but you have been so gracious that still I dare to be bold—do you think I could prevail upon you to remove this bandage? I am sure even the learned Doctor Fell would agree that it has been on long enough, don't you think?''

He held his breath as he waited for Aunt Lucinda to stop dithering and come to a decision. Finally, when he thought she must have fallen asleep, he felt her fingers struggling with the knots, and in a few moments he was blinking against the sudden return of light.

''Bless you, madam,'' he breathed in real gratitude, rapidly opening and closing his eyes experimentally several times. ''I had begun to despair of ever again seeing our watery English sun.'' Then he looked at the woman, trying his best to school his expression into one resembling that of his childhood hound, Bruno, who had owned the saddest face in nature. ''Indeed, Aunt Lucinda, you see before you a man who is nearly overcome with woe and deepest despair.''

Aunt Lucinda only smiled at him knowingly, quipping, '' 'Where be your gibes now? your gambols? your songs?

your flashes of merriment that were wont to set the table on a roar?' Shakespeare.''

The Earl allowed his breath to hiss through his clenched teeth. "So you're in on it, too, Mrs. Benedict? Or should I be saying, *'Et tu, Brute'* in my best schoolboy Greek? Why then, may I ask, are you here at all? Surely a lady such as yourself is above gloating.''

Making a great business out of unfolding her fine, embroidered lawn handkerchief and dabbing it carefully against the corners of her brightly painted mouth, Aunt Lucinda replied with patent dishonesty. " 'I would bring balm and pour it into your wound, cure your distemper'd mind and heal your fortunes,' Dryden.''

"Balm, is it? Strange. It feels much like salt to me,'' Lucien mocked, turning his head away from her. "How much longer am I to be punished? I'll admit it, I deserve everything that's been done to me, but my patience runs thin.'' He would have added that he had begun to believe the Marquess was on his way, and a marriage between he and Lady Penelope was all but an accomplished fact, but he restrained himself. After all, if the idea had not as yet occurred to Aunt Lucinda, he wasn't about to make her a gift of it. Instead, he only said, "You know who I really am, don't you? That's the only reason I can find for my treatment.''

" 'One ear heard it, and at the other out it went,' Chaucer.'' Clearly Aunt Lucinda wasn't about to admit to anything. His estimation of her intelligence rose in accordance with his drop in spirit.

"Very well, if that's the way you wish to play it,'' Lucien agreed resignedly, turning once more to face her as he tried another approach. "I lied. I am not Lucas Kendall. I am Lucien Kendrick, Earl of Leighton, a member of one of the oldest, most distinguished houses in England. In plain words, your captive, madam, is a very important person.''

" 'A fool, indeed, has great need of a title; it teaches men to call him count and duke, and to forget his proper name of fool,' Crowne,'' Aunt Lucinda warned him, wagging one beringed finger beneath his nose as she rose to her feet, in preparation of quitting the room.

"Please don't leave, Aunt Lucinda," Lucien pleaded even as he wondered why he wished she would stay. "I didn't mean to be arrogant, truly I didn't. I can't imagine what came over me. Please forgive me."

" 'A toad-eater's an imp I don't admire,' Wolcot," was all Aunt Lucinda said, lifting her skirts carefully until she had passed back around the bottom edge of the bed, as if she hadn't wanted to contaminate herself.

She had learned all that she needed to know. The Earl was still a long way from being ready to admit what she was sure was in his heart. She wasn't very disappointed, for she hadn't expected to find him prostrate on a bed of guilt, calling for her niece with an offer of marriage in mind.

After all, no man really understands his own heart. It takes time, time and careful planning, to bring gentlemen of independent ilk up to the sticking point. The Dowager had taught her that. For now she would content herself with the sure knowledge that the Earl of Leighton was on the hook, and although still fighting for his freedom, was nearly ready to be reeled in to shore.

"Wait!" Lucien called after her, anxious not to lose his only ally, if Aunt Lucinda could truly be called that. "Won't you please reconsider? A pretty fool I am at that, and in no position to be asking favors, I grant you. But, please, come back and sit with me, at least until Farnley appears with my gruel—Oh, damn and blast, she's gone!"

Lucien was left alone again for nearly an hour, an hour during which he alternately ranted and raved at his deplorable situation and patiently worked on loosening the binding around his right wrist, which showed signs of coming loose, before Farnley arrived bearing some insipid runny porridge that the Earl refused to eat, saying the butler would have to do more than truss him up and blindfold him to get him to voluntarily take poison.

"Poison?" Farnley cried, aghast. "Oh, no, m'lord, never poison. I told 'em I wouldn't be a party to that. It was only a bit of poppy flower in your rabbit stew, I swear it, and I only did that to keep you from getting brain fever from Mrs. Benedict's silly prattlings. Please, m'lord, if I leave the blindfold off, won't you understand that I have to obey my orders? I'd let you go in a minute, really I would, but they'd know it was me and then they'd turn me off without a notice—me and dearest Pansy—and where would we be then, I ask you? With you run off someplace and no help to us, we'd be sleeping among the hedgerows—me, who's got all the way up to butler's keys. Please, m'lord, have pity on me.''

"Pity on you?'' Lucien jibed, laughing in spite of himself at the sight of the agitated little man. "I'm tied naked to a bed, with no hope of escape, while that lovable widget Aunt Lucinda spouts bad poetry at me and the butler weeps into my porridge—only *after* drugging my rabbit, mind you—and you want me to feel sorry for *you?* What's even more surprising, I think I actually *am* sorry for you, Farnley, for indeed, you are the sorriest human being it has ever been my misfortune to meet. Now hie your sniveling self out of here before I am completely unmanned by your plight and find myself bursting into womanish tears!''

Farnley fled as fast as his thin, bandy legs would carry him, leaving Lucien once more alone and growing increasingly ravenous, which probably explained the longing look he directed at the cold chicken leg that soon appeared in the room, and why he paid so little attention to the fashionably dressed young man carrying it.

"Whoops!'' Cyril said, hastily stepping back a pace when he spied out the Earl looking in his direction. "I thought they said your eyes was covered? Oh well, I guess it's too late anyway, now that you've seen me. I'm Cyril Rayburn, by the way—Penny's brother. I helped strip you down and tie you up the other night.''

"Really? How exciting for you,'' Lucien commented, still staring at the half-eaten poultry.

Cyril interrupted his introduction long enough to take another healthy bite of the chicken leg. "Yes. It was accomplished simply enough though, since that opium already had you sleeping like a babe. I wanted to hang you up from the pub sign in the village square with nary a stitch on you, but Cosmo shot me down. Pity. This was all right for a while, but we'll have to let you go sooner or later, won't we? They should have thought of that.''

Lucien stared at the young man, remarking silently on his close resemblance to Philip, both physically and in his

124

open, friendly, and somewhat dim-witted manner. "Who's Cosmo?" he asked at last, when Lord Rayburn's confession ran down.

"M'brother. We're twins, you know. Surely Philippos must have told you. We saw you last year in London at some rout or other; only I guess you didn't see us, because most people remember. We look deucedly alike, you see, Cosmo and me." He thrust out his bottom lip, deciding whether or not he should be insulted by this oversight, then decided to let it go. "The room *was* fairly crowded— what Philippos says is called a crush—so I guess I can't blame you."

"That's awfully decent of you, Cyril," Lucien replied, hiding a smile. "So you and—Cosmo, was it?—are the people I have to thank for my current predicament. You said it wasn't your idea, so I'll assume it is Cosmo who came up with such a brilliant plan. Not many minds would even dare consider trussing up an Earl."

Cyril dropped easily into the chair beside the bed, his long legs sprawled out in front of him. "You're wrong there, you know," he supplied cheerfully, wiping at his chin with the back of one hand. "Our sister Penny thought it up all by herself. She's a real gun with a prank, Penny is, and this one thrilled her right down to her toes. Not that she's crowing too loud this morning, of course. Hasn't been ever since Cosmo told her she has to marry you."

"Marry me?" Lucien prompted, hearing his worst fear confirmed.

"Yes," Cyril agreed easily. "I told him Penny wouldn't stand still for it, but Cosmo says it has to be that way. He's probably right, too. Cosmo's the bright twin, you see." He held the half-eaten chicken leg out to the Earl. "Here. Want a bite? No, I guess not. You're all tied up at the moment, aren't you? *Ha!* I think I made a joke. 'All tied up at the moment'—oh, I say, that's rich!"

"Enjoying yourself, brother?" Cosmo asked, entering the room, a frown on his face.

It's beginning to get crowded in here, Lucien decided ruefully as Cosmo sat down familiarly on the bottom of the bed. "If you ring the bell," the Earl growled, "I'm sure we can convince Farnley to bring up some refreshments. Really, sirs, make yourselves comfortable. I'm always at home to callers on Tuesdays. This *is* Tuesday, isn't it?''

Cyril carelessly tossed the denuded chicken leg onto a nearby table while he chuckled at Lucien's dry wit. "He's a bit of all right, ain't he, Cosmo? He's even making jokes. Can't we cut him loose now? After all, Penny's locked in her rooms all right and tight.''

Lucien looked from one twin to the other, noticing the flush that had invaded Cosmo's cheeks. "You locked Lady Penelope Rayburn in her rooms? I'd rather try to tame a wild lion with a riding crop. My congratulations, gentlemen. You're much more courageous than I would have believed.''

"Cosmo here caught her tippytoeing down the hall last night with a sewing shears in her hand,'' Cyril supplied, preening a bit at this praise. "She somehow got it into her head that if she cut you loose, you'd lope off and she wouldn't have to marry you as soon as Papa arrives. Cosmo sent a note off to him this morning, you understand, telling him all about it. As if we wouldn't know where to find you if you was to make a break for it. Silly girl.''

"Cyril.''

Cyril turned to look at his brother inquiringly. "Yes, Cosmo?''

"Shut up, Cyril,'' Cosmo said succinctly, effectively wiping the pleased smile from his brother's face.

"I didn't tell him anything he won't find out sooner or later,'' Cyril said, pouting and continuing to speak as if Lucien weren't in the room. "Penny told us he compromised her, so they have to be married. You said so. Told her so, too—which is why the poor dear is locked in her rooms, breathing fire.''

"She doesn't want to marry me?'' Lucien frowned, trying to understand why this knowledge, which should have lent him some small comfort, bothered him.

"I guess you could say that,'' Cyril quipped, "seeing as how she flew straight up into the boughs the minute Cosmo pointed it out to her. I don't think Penny likes you very much, sir, to tell you the truth. Sorry.''

Lucien looked from one twin to the other, then shifted his bound body slightly on the bed in an effort to make himself more comfortable. "Doubtless I shall go into a sad decline," he said, pretending weariness with the subject of Lady Penelope's poor opinion of him. "Tell me, am I to remain tied up here until she has a change of heart, or will Lady Penelope and I both be dragged to the altar at swordpoint? As far as weddings go, it lacks something for romance, I feel bound to point out, but then who am I to cavil, miserable creature that I am? After all, I have already been cast in the role of a hardened seducer of innocent maidens, haven't I?"

"I don't think I like what you're inferring. You kissed her! Penny wouldn't lie to us about such a thing!" Cyril declared angrily, rising to his feet, all sympathy for the Earl having disappeared with these last words. "Let me tell you, it's a lucky thing for you that you're tied up, sirrah, or else I should be tempted to call you out."

After watching his brother stomp heavily out of the room, his chin in the air—probably to head straight for Aunt Lucinda and some tender sympathy—Cosmo took his place in the chair beside the bed, saying blandly, "You're making quite a few friends during your stay here in Wormhill, aren't you, sir? With that velvet tongue of yours, I can see why you're known as the toast of London."

"I don't like that you have locked Lady Penelope away in her room," Lucien complained, surprising himself. Once he had begun to speak, he decided to go the whole route, saying, "She *is* totally innocent in this, you know. I did trick her, take advantage of her. I did compromise her. I'm not proud of it, but I did it, knowing full well she was Philip's sister. Cyril has every right to hate me, as you do. But do you really think you should punish Lady Penelope for being a victim?"

Cosmo debated with himself for a few moments, considering Lucien's words. Penny wasn't happy, it didn't take a prize scholar to figure that out, but what else was he to do? Her honor had been tarnished, the entire Rayburn family had been insulted, and the only remedy was to have the Earl and his sister wed as soon as possible. Surely his sister would come to realize that—once she had calmed down and stopped throwing vases at his head each time he tried to enter her chamber. Even Doreen was on his side, whispering something to him about the first drop of the broth being the hottest, and that her mistress would soon learn to swallow the idea.

If he could only get the picture of his sister's sad, tear-streaked, little face out of his mind, he'd feel easier about the whole thing. Oh, he knew she was up to her old tricks, blatantly playing on his sympathies so that he'd order her door unlocked, whereupon she would go hotfooting to the Earl's chamber and set him free, but that didn't mean he was entirely invulnerable to her woebegone expression and impassioned pleas for assistance.

If only Papa would arrive soon so he could dump all this awesome responsibility onto older and wiser shoulders. Aunt Lucinda was less than no help at all, walking about with that inane smile on her face, and spouting random verses from *The Taming of the Shrew*.

"I can't do it," Cosmo said at last, looking to Lucien for understanding. "She'd only sneak in here tonight and set you free. Penny's like that, you know."

All the time the twins had been in the room, Lucien had been working on loosening the bindings holding his right wrist, and he had felt his hand come free in time to wave that appendage at Cyril in farewell if he had so chosen.

Now he pushed back the coverlet and held up his unencumbered hand to Cosmo, saying confidingly, "If I had chosen to lope off, my friend, I could have easily conked you over the head with that candelabra sitting beside me minutes ago and then been on my merry way. However, although I have already admitted to my sins against your sister, I have not sunk so low that I would turn my back on my own perverted sense of right and wrong. I do have some honor left to me. Now, kind sir, if you would bring me back my clothes and release your sister, I will endeavor to make her understand why we should become betrothed—preferably before the Marquess arrives. I shan't try to escape."

Lady Penelope was in the drawing room an hour later, pacing up and down the length of the Aubusson carpet at a rate that would have made most young ladies breathless, her small hands gathered into tight fists at her sides. Her unbound hair billowed around her shoulders as she walked, the fiery gold curls bouncing up and down in rhythm with her firm, determined steps as if they had taken on a life of their own. Angry color had turned her cheeks to palest peach, and her emerald eyes (now most lamentably narrowed into evil-looking slits) glittered like hard stones. The skirts of her sunshine yellow morning gown foamed about her ankles, and she kicked at them furiously whenever they dared to tangle around her legs.

She was incensed and taking no pains to hide the fact.

She was also heartstoppingly beautiful and totally unaware of that beauty.

Lucien stood in the doorway, admiring the young woman at his leisure as he carefully adjusted his shirt cuffs below the sleeves of his finely tailored mustard-gold jacket. He lightly touched a hand to his cravat, assuring himself that it was still arranged in the simple perfection he had achieved with the admiring Cyril and Cosmo looking on in openmouthed awe, and then advanced into the room, his injured ankle causing him to limp only slightly.

"You're still in residence, then," he said urbanely, by way of a greeting. "I had rather expected you to have hopped aboard that huge grey gelding you ride and run away like a Minerva Press heroine who has just been told she is about to suffer a Fate Worse Than Death. What a pity; I'm disappointed in you. I should think I'd like another chance to match my Hades against your mount, although I should insist upon first examining the course, as I find I have recently developed quite an aversion to stone walls."

Lady Penelope had stopped her furious pacing and slowly turned in his direction as he spoke, her demurely muslin-draped bosom drawing his admiring attention as it rose and fell rapidly in her agitation. *"You!"* she ejaculated accusingly, glaring at him. He was still the most handsome, elegant man she had ever seen, and she hated him more with every breath she drew.

The Earl smiled deprecatingly and executed a graceful leg in her direction. "Lucien Kenrick at your service, my lady. However, I would appreciate it if you would please seat your sweet self down somewhere, as I would then be able to rest my ankle without fear that you were about to launch an assault on my person.''

''I wouldn't waste my time on such a sniveling coward as yourself,'' Lady Penelope countered, nevertheless walking across the carpet to plunk herself down on one corner of the satin settee.

''Coward?'' Lucien repeated archly, gingerly seating himself at the opposite end of the settee and resting his ankle on a nearby footstool. ''Ah, that's better.''

''Yes, coward!'' Lady Penelope crowed, turning on the settee to face him. ''I'll say it again. Coward, coward, *coward!* You didn't even put up a fight, did you? How *dare* you tell my brothers that you'll marry me?''

Lucien lowered his head slightly as he reached to scratch at his temple, hiding the smile that had involuntarily sprung to his lips. Obviously the lady was not pleased.

''Well?'' Are you just going to sit there like a lump?'' Lady Penelope pushed on, longing to do the man an injury. How could she ever have worried that she was attracted to such a man? ''Don't you have anything to say for yourself? After all, it's you who got us into this mess.''

Now Lucien did look at her, his mobile left eyebrow arching high on his forehead. ''Oh, really? I suppose it was *I* who went running to *my* brothers with the sordid tale of how you threw yourself onto my bed of pain and all but ravished me? How remiss of me; it must have slipped my mind—probably somewhere between nibbling drugged rabbit and awakening to find myself tied to my bed.''

''How was I supposed to know you were the Earl of Leighton?'' Lady Penelope argued belligerently, inelegantly tucking one leg under her as she leaned forward to make her point. ''I thought you were Lucas Kendall, *a married man,* and I wanted to have my brothers help me move you out of the house before my father could show up—which he is sure to do because the twins left Weybridge without permission—and learn that I'd gotten myself into another scrape, which would put me in the basket for certain because then I would have lost the wager and have had to agree to a London Season, not that *that* is any of your business, for it is not.''

''Naturally, however—'' Leighton tried to interrupt, but to no avail, as Lady Penelope was not about to let him get a rebuttal in sideways.

''Of course, if Cosmo hadn't been prattling on and on about the Pettibone—as if I couldn't possibly have anything even the *least* bit shocking to say after being stuck away here at Wormhill—I probably never would have mentioned the kiss at all. And if you hadn't lied to me, making me think you were married and embarrassed to have been attracted to me when you couldn't recall who you were, while I found myself—well, never mind about that! I would *never* have told Cyril and Cosmo that you kissed me. I'm not that much of a zany that I wouldn't have eventually realized that Cosmo would figure out that I had been compromised and then be so straitlaced as to demand we be wed. And I didn't drug your stupid rabbit, Farnley did.''

''Oh, I see,'' Lucien said, nodding his head as if he understood, while secretly marveling that anyone could say that much so quickly without having to stop for breath. So he had been right in one thing at least—his kiss hadn't left her totally unaffected. ''Let me see if I have got this correct. If you had known who I *really* was before blurting out that interesting information concerning my stolen kiss, you would have merely asked Cosmo and Cyril to remove me from the premises and never mentioned our little interlude, is that right?''

''Yes!''

''As a matter of fact,'' he continued, smiling in spite of himself, ''I might then have awakened yesterday afternoon to find myself swinging naked in the breeze in front of a covey of interested villagers—if I remember Cyril's sentiments correctly. No, wait, I imagine not. Please forgive me, as I grow confused. I would have merely been banished to a safe distance, like an annoying but harmless pest, and not punished at all. Oh, yes, and you didn't drug my rabbit. Farnley did. Do I have it all straight now?''

Lady Penelope sagged back in her seat as she answered tiredly, ''Exactly, although it all sounds so—so sordid when you say it like that. So you see, the entire thing is your fault. Yours and Philippos'—I mean, Philip's.''

''Philip? You think Philip is in on this?''

''Isn't he?''

Lucien rubbed his chin thoughtfully, once more considering this possibility. ''No, not really, at least not directly. He did tell me you were residing in the neighborhood for the winter, but he took great pains to push home to me the fact that you and I should never suit. You really might see if the boy needs spectacles, or else his powers of observation are sadly remiss. Ask him to describe your features one day. Anyway, as it was, I only came upon you by accident, having taken a wrong turning near Buxton on my way north. If he hasn't shown up here since my arrival, I'd have to conclude that the fellow is innocent of any wrongdoing.''

Rising once more to her feet, Lady Penelope set to pacing again while considering the Earl's last words. She hadn't really believed Philippos to be behind the scheme, although he had known she was to be staying at Wormhill and could have sent Lucien to her. Stopping in front of Leighton, who was eyeing her feet carefully as he held out his hands as if to protect his injured ankle, she agreed austerely, ''So Philippos is innocent. That still does not explain why you shamelessly feigned that loss of memory, for I know now that your illness was all a sham.''

''Not quite entirely a sham, my dear, and I have the bruises to prove it. Consider the thing from my side for a moment. I was alone and injured and in a strange place,'' Lucien pointed out, carefully shifting his injured ankle onto the settee. ''I wished to check out the lay of the land, as it were, before disclosing my identity. Once I deduced, and correctly as it turned out, that you were Philip's sister, I decided to remain anonymous as—how shall I put this?— I wasn't particularly anxious to have you summoning your dear brother to my bedside if, indeed, you did know his direction. He is staying at a house party not far from here, you know.''

''But my brother is your friend,'' Lady Penelope remarked, confused. ''Why wouldn't you want him here?

And don't call me 'my dear,' " she added scrupulously, wishing she could ignore his easy charm.

Now Lucien smiled engagingly, causing Lady Penelope's stomach to flutter against her will. "Sad to say, you are not the only person who plays pranks. When last I saw dear Philip, he was comfortably tucked up, snoring away in Lord Crompton's larder beside a rather large salmon. I did not wish to be exposed to Philip just then, while I was all but helpless."

"Philippos sleeping with a salmon? How angry he must have been when he awoke!" Lady Penelope exclaimed, trying hard to keep a straight face as she pictured her brother reduced to such circumstances. "He can't abide the things."

"Yes, so he said. You can see my dilemma," Lucien retorted, grinning up at her, and then they both laughed, easing the tension in the room for a few moments.

But this relief did not last long, for it wasn't many minutes before Lady Penelope remembered that, no matter what circumstances had brought them to this stage, there was still the matter of their betrothal to discuss. "I won't marry you, you know," she said finally, settling herself on the now vacant footstool. "I have vowed never to marry." Her words resounded hollowly in her ears, as if she were merely repeating an oft-stated remark and not really convinced of its merit. "Never!" she added quickly, to make her point.

"Then we do have something in common other than our sad proclivity toward pranking, my lady," Lucien pointed out, sobering, "for I, too, have resolved never to wed."

Lady Penelope raised her palms toward him in exasperation. "Now I'm thoroughly confused! Then why have you told Cosmo that you and I should become betrothed? You know, for an Earl, you really don't make a great deal of sense."

Lucien leaned forward to chuck her gently beneath the chin. "As your dear Aunt Lucinda might say, 'There is many a slip 'twixt the cup and the lip,' Palladas."

"Meaning?" Lady Penelope asked hurriedly, feeling hopeful at last. She wanted Lucien Kenrick out of her life as soon as possible. He was a dangerous, dangerous man, complicating her life and making her doubt her own mind. All her resolve to remain independent seemed to melt like snowflakes in the hot sun at his slightest touch.

"Meaning, my dear prankster, that between us, we should certainly be able to convince your family that a union between the two of us is the very last thing any sane person would desire."

"In other words, if we don't fight the betrothal, but merely proceed with it, and then show how much havoc we could cause as a pair, Papa and my brothers will eventually beg us to call it all off? Would that satisfy their ridiculous male honor?" And allow me to return to my beloved Weybridge where I can forget this maddening man even exists? she added silently.

"It would," Lucien promised, hoping he was right.

"My Lord Leighton," Lady Penelope replied sweetly, bravely holding out her right hand to seal their bargain, "I do believe you begin to interest me. Please consider your kind offer of marriage accepted. Now, precisely what do you have in mind for our opening salvo?"

Chapter Eleven

C YRIL was reclining at his ease on a comfortable French corner chair in the drawing room after dinner, Aunt Lucinda hovering nearby as had become her custom, anticipating his every need, feeding him refreshments, and even offering to turn the pages of the sporting magazine he was leafing through to relieve his boredom.

Not since dear Jerome had gone to his heavenly reward had the woman felt so overwhelmingly happy, for once more she had someone to cosset and fuss over, someone who appreciated her attentions (not that Jerome had stayed home for more than a few days at a time between his gambling engagements, usually leaving in a rush, muttering some nonsense under his breath about being smothered).

Raising his gaze from the magazine for a moment, Cyril looked toward his brother, who was pacing up and down the carpet, his hands opening and closing spasmodically behind his back, and showing all the signs of an old hen fretting over her only chick.

"Oh, Cosmo, sit down, do," Cyril begged. "You're making Aunt Lucinda and me dizzy with all this to-ing and fro-ing. I'd have thought you'd be over the moon, with Penny and Lord Leighton billing and cooing at each other over the turbot this evening. Getting awfully like Papa, that's what you are, always looking for trouble. Bad sign, that—you might even be growing up. Really, Cosmo, it's most depressing."

Cosmo stopped his pacing to look across at his brother in disgust. "You're deader than a red brick, you know that, Cyril? Sometimes you actually make me ashamed to call you brother. Haven't you learned by now that the worst—the very worst—sign is Penny behaving herself? What's she up to? That's what I want to know.''

'' 'Double, double toil and trouble; fire burn and cauldron bubble,' Shakes—''

"Thank you, ma'am," Cosmo cut in wearily, dropping onto a nearby chair, "but I think perhaps you should quote instead from a few lines farther along in Macbeth: 'By the pricking of my thumbs, something wicked this way comes.' She's up to something, Cyril, mark my words. It isn't like Penny to be so amenable. Lord, she was almost sickening in her sweetness tonight. Anyone would think we've granted her fondest wish, forcing her to wed Leighton.''

Aunt Lucinda just gave a dismissive toss of her curls, sure that Cosmo was grasping at straws. The Earl and her niece were betrothed, just as she had hoped for from the very start. All the struggles were behind them now, and she saw no reason not to rejoice. Soon the Marquess would arrive—thanks to her timely letter—and the engagement would become official. She could hardly wait for the day the notice appeared in the London papers, and she could send off a clipping to the Dowager. No, there was no reason for concern. Everything was moving along just swimmingly.

Cyril, who either shared his aunt's sentiments or had just tired of the conversation, buried his head once more in his magazine, trying to fathom the intricacies of tying the Fitzgerald Ultimate Precision Fishing Lure that was featured in one of its articles.

That left only the uneasy Cosmo to carry the burden of his suspicions. He sat on the edge of his chair, nervously worrying on the side of his right thumb with his teeth as he stared out into the dark, denuded garden, into which Lady Penelope and the Earl, walking arm in arm most companionably, had disappeared immediately after dessert.

"I still don't see why you had to hold my hand that way under the table," Lady Penelope was complaining as she sat down on a cold stone bench and drew her heavy, fur-lined cloak more closely around her. "After all, it wasn't as if anyone could see us."

Lucien stood in front of her on the narrow brick path, looking down at the halo of curls that glistened in the light of the full moon. "Farnley noticed when he served the soup. As he undoubtably reports everything he sees to your Aunt Lucinda, I saw it as necessary to our plan. Everyone must be made to believe the two of us truly want this engagement. It's the only way for our plan to succeed. Believe me, I don't like it any more than you do."

At his last words, Lady Penelope's head shot up and she glared at him angrily. "I think you've already made your dislike for me abundantly clear, my lord. There's no need to belabor the point, is there?"

Lucien sat down beside her and took one of her chilled hands in his, holding it firmly against his chest as she tried to pull away. "You misunderstood, Lady Penelope," he said slowly. "I don't dislike you at all. Witness my lapse of a few days past if you doubt me. You are a very beautiful, very appealing young woman, and I find myself greatly attracted to you. Did you, for instance, know that you have the most kissable lips I've ever seen? You do, you know. *That's* why I find my role so difficult to play."

Lady Penelope bent her head slightly toward her breast as she slipped her shoulder closer to his body and peeped at him out of the corners of her eyes. "Really?" she asked, pleased in spite of herself.

"Oh-ho!" Lucien said, laughing as he gave her captured hand a quick squeeze. "The lady has all the fine moves of a dedicated flirt. Shame on you, Lady Penelope; and I thought you said you had no interest in men."

The shoulder and hand were immediately withdrawn as Lady Penelope quickly put a full two feet of space between their bodies. "You're despicable!" she accused, turning to face the overgrown evergreen that stood beside the end of the bench. "And I don't care a bent farthing what you think of my lips—I mean, what you think of me. Just tell me how you expect us to break this engagement. So far, your plan only seems to be making our trouble all the worse. Why can't we just go on showing everyone how much we hate each other? It's so much easier to be natural.''

Lucien ignored her jibe and slipped a hand inside his coat, withdrawing a thin silver flask from an inside pocket. Unscrewing the top, he then held the bottle out to her. ''Have you ever tasted brandy, my dear?'' he asked, waving the open flask under her nose.

Just the aroma of the strong spirit caused a shiver to run through her upper body, and she pushed the flask away, saying, ''Once when I had the bellyache Papa made me drink some of the horrid stuff. I thought my throat had caught on fire. Besides, what has brandy to do with anything?''

Pouring a portion of brandy into the deep cap that had been specially fashioned for that purpose, Lucien downed the measure of fiery liquor, then smiled at her mischievously. ''All right then, have you any idea of my reputation, Lady Penelope?'' he asked, refilling the cap with another generous amount of liquid. ''I am considered to be quite incorrigible, truth to tell, always up to some sort of mischief. For instance, it wouldn't be at all past a hey-go-mad scamp like myself to introduce my willing fiancée to the evils of brandy.''

Lady Penelope looked at the silver cap for a moment before a slow, comprehending smile lit her features. ''Papa would have a fit if I were ever to appear the worse for drink,'' she said, biting her bottom lip as she gingerly took the cap from his hand. ''But as I love my betrothed so dearly, I would do anything he desired, wouldn't I? Oh, dear, what a lamentably bad influence you are on an impressionable young girl, my lord. You should be ashamed of yourself.''

The Earl watched as Lady Penelope lifted the cap to her lips, squeezed her eyes shut as if she were about to be dosed with a particularly vile medicine, and finally drained its contents in one long gulp. Pulling the cap out of her hand, he clapped her soundly on the back as she began at once to sputter and choke on two generous fingers of what he considered to be the smoothest brandy in England.

''Here, here,'' he protested, laughing, ''I never said you should drink the stuff. I only wanted you to wet your mouth with it, so that your brothers would smell it on your breath when we go back inside to say good night. You don't need to *be* drunk to act the part, do you?''

Blinking back the sharp, stinging tears that had invaded her eyes, Lady Penelope swallowed down hard and swiveled on the bench to look at the Earl. ''I once saw Cosmo and Cyril after they had gotten into Papa's best port one Sunday morning when they'd stayed home, saying they were too ill to attend church. Papa and I arrived home to find them hanging headfirst over the first floor balcony doing something very nasty into the flower beds. Their faces were the most dreadful shade of green, too,'' she added thoughtfully. ''The poor dears were sick for two days. I shan't have to do that, shall I?''

Lucien chuckled softly. ''You won't be required to take things to such lengths, my dear,'' he assured her. ''A slight slurring of your speech, an occasional stumble in your walk—these should be sufficient to show your protective brothers that I am pointing your dainty toes straight down the path to perdition.''

The brandy she had gulped down suddenly hit Lady Penelope's bloodstream, and she could feel a cozy warmth growing in her chest. It was silly, but suddenly she was feeling very much in charity toward the Earl. Tilting her head to one side, she smiled at him and said, ''May I giggle, too, my lord? I don't usually, you understand, for I think it to be odiously missish, but I really do think I should like to giggle.''

And then she did.

''Oh, my God!'' Lucien exclaimed in sudden understanding, putting out a hand to hold her upright as her body slowly began to sag against his. ''I forgot all about those two glasses of wine you had at dinner. You shan't have to fake it, my dear little souse, you *are* drunk!''

''Am not!'' Lady Penelope answered proudly, opening her emerald eyes very wide before poking Lucien in the center of his chest with one carefully aimed fingertip. ''Now you say 'are too,' like Cosmo and Cyril used to do. Go ahead. It's a very funny game.'' As if to prove her point, she tipped back her head, crowed, ''are too,'' and then artlessly rested her head against his shoulder. "Goodness, I'm dizzy."

Shifting his body slightly so that he could better balance her relaxed weight against his side, Lucien raised his gaze to the full moon, thinking the old man who lived there was looking down on them, smiling at his delicate predicament. "Now what do I do?" he asked the distant voyeur, trying very hard not to think about the provocative way Lady Penelope's soft breast curved against his chest.

All the physical urgings he had experienced while lying in his sickbed—the amorous, vaguely nefarious thoughts he'd entertained while watching his beautiful nurse tend to his needs—resurfaced with a vengeance, making it difficult for him to breathe and even harder for him to remember he wanted nothing more to do with this glorious, intriguing woman-child than to be shed of her as quickly as possible, and thus relieved of the complications her accidental advent into his life had caused.

She was an Innocent, an unawakened, unknowing, totally unaware Innocent, and she was more dangerous than any enemy he had ever faced across a battlefield.

His mind fought a swift, savage battle with his body; his common sense declaring war on his sudden, overwhelming need to feel her warm, willing lips once more beneath his questing mouth; her soft, warm body once more pressed close against his hard, straining muscles.

In this way of thinking lay madness, his mind told him reasonably, and for a short while his better self, his saner self, held the field.

He had not, however, sufficient reserves of willpower to repel a sneak attack.

His first inkling that he was engaged in fighting a losing battle came when Lady Penelope's cold little hand, instinctively searching out the warmth that lay beneath his open coat, tucked itself against his upper belly, kneading his silk-covered skin like a kitten preparing to settle itself for a nap. He could feel the involuntary rippling of his muscles as his breath caught painfully in his throat.

Even then he might have saved the day, had Lady Penelope not chosen that moment to look up at him with her brandy-bleared eyes and ask, "You really think my lips

140

are kissable?'' After running the tip of her tongue across her upper lip from one side to the other, licking at the remnants of brandy that clung there, she added, ''Nobody ever said that to me before, you know. I believe I should thank you. Thank you,'' she said politely, her smile soft and dreamy.

''Oh, damn!'' Lucien breathed hoarsely, mentally waving the white flag of surrender as he used his free hand to tip up her chin before he closed his mind and his eyes, and gave himself over to the unbelievable ecstasy of her mouth.

''Stop that at once!''

Lucien lifted his head, startled, and turned himself toward the sound of snapping, cracking shrubbery in time to see Cosmo Rayburn groping his way through the underbrush as he recklessly pelted toward the small clearing, disregarding the winding path and uncaring of the damage being done to his new evening coat.

''I knew there'd be trouble,'' Cosmo was saying as a thin branch whipped across his cheek, leaving an angry welt. ''Ouch! Damn it all, anyway! 'Leave them alone,' Cyril said. ' ''Love's young dream,'' ' Aunt Lucinda quoted. Hah! Penny, sit up, for the Lord's sake, and straighten your cloak! What if Papa were to see you? *Penny!''*

Lady Penelope heard her voice being called as if from a great distance. Blinking furiously, she struggled to focus her eyes on the large dark shape that hovered over her menacingly, but it was too much of an effort, and she allowed her head to rest once more on Lucien's shoulder. ''Go 'way,'' she ordered, waving her hand carelessly in the direction of the voice before tucking it back under Lucien's coat.

''You're slurring quite nicely, pet,'' Lucien whispered into her ear, somehow seeing some humor in the thing, although he could have cheerfully strangled Cosmo for interrupting him. ''Shall we see how you walk?''

Cosmo's eyes appeared to have popped halfway out of his handsome young face. ''She's drunk!'' he exclaimed, slapping the palms of his hands against his forehead in exasperation. ''You've gotten my sister drunk, you—you *cad!*

"Oh, grow up, Cosmo," Lucien ordered nastily, re-membering the point of the exercise. "She's going to be my wife soon. I can't have a baby for a bride. Penny's going to have to learn to hold her spirits if she's going to live with me."

"Oh, hello, Cosmo," Lady Penelope interrupted hap-pily, finally understanding that her brother had arrived on the scene. She raised her head, and it waved about like a heavy, red-gold blossom on a slender stem as she smiled up at him. "I feel delicious. Ab-so-lute-ly *de-e-e*-licious."

"Isn't she just darling, Cosmo?" Lucien said, visibly preening as he planted a loud kiss on Lady Penelope's cheek. "My friends in Paris are all going to love her."

"Paris?" Cosmo choked, aghast. "Penny's not going to Paris. Papa says the place is completely decadent."

Lucien helped Lady Penelope to her feet, noticing as he did that she was becoming increasingly stiff in his arms, alerting him to the fact that her brandy-induced friendli-ness was soon to become a thing of the past. "Your Papa is not going to have anything to say about it, is he, my dear soon-to-be brother-in-law?"

"I want Doreen," Lady Penelope whined now in a small voice, holding a hand to her mouth. "I don't think I feel very well."

"Of course you don't, you idiot girl!" Cosmo agreed shrilly, taking hold of her arm with some force and leading her, stumbling and weaving, up the path toward the glass doors to the drawing room. "You smell to high heaven of brandy. I can't believe you let him do this to you."

Neither can I, Lady Penelope thought inwardly, not so cupshot that she couldn't remember the searing kiss that had passed between her and Lucien not two minutes ear-lier. Why is it that every time I get within ten feet of that man, I turn into a mindless idiot? I hate him!

She almost said as much to Cosmo as he and Cyril helped her to her rooms, but remembered Lucien's in-structions in time to mumble quietly, "Dearest Lucien, I do love him so," before her brothers gratefully handed her over to Doreen's clucking ministrations.

Later, tucked up in her bed with a warm brick at her

chilled toes, Lady Penelope wondered why of all things she could have said, she had said what she had.

Lucien stayed on in the dark garden for a long time after Cosmo and Lady Penelope had gone, thoughtfully smoking a long, thin cheroot and taking an occasional warmth-restoring sip from his decanter of brandy as he sat pondering the events of the previous half hour.

He wasn't feeling particularly proud of himself, as well he might not be, for he had just done a very despicable thing. He had plied a beautiful young woman with strong spirits and then shamelessly taken advantage of her when she didn't have all her wits about her. It hadn't exactly been the action of an upstanding gentleman.

Even worse, he rued painfully as he punished himself with his reminiscences, he had thoroughly enjoyed the entire sordid episode. Lady Penelope was the most kissable young woman he had ever encountered, just as he had admitted to her earlier—although he had told himself at the time that the only reason he had said such a thing was to keep her amenable to his plans to sabotage their engagement. Oh yes, he had been a real, first-class bounder, using the situation for his own gain.

Yet he smiled in spite of himself as he recalled how appealing Lady Penelope had appeared in her altitudes, believing that even while slightly in her cups, she was still the most beautiful child he'd ever before chanced to encounter. If he had been on the hunt for a wife, he couldn't imagine another female who so well suited him—not that he was interested in marriage, for he was not.

Lucien's lips thinned as he conjured up a mental picture of Ann Louise, the bride he had taken at the ridiculously young age of eighteen. How gullible he had been, how completely and stupidly infatuated.

Well, he thought now as he had so many years ago, I won't be caught in that trap twice! If I've learned anything, I've learned not to trust in happily ever afters.

Yes, you learned, his conscience agreed, but do you really think you can compare Ann Louise with Lady Penelope?

"A woman's a woman," Lucien dully declared aloud

into the quiet night. "My mother, Ann Louise, Philip's Dorinda Redfern, Penelope—they're all the same."

Are they? a little nagging voice inside his weary brain asked quietly as he dropped his head into his hands. Are they truly all the same? Even Penny?

"Where is she? Take me to her at once, I command you! Damn it all man, why are you standing there like you was stuffed? Where's my daughter?"

Farnley battled free of the heavy cloak that, moments earlier, had enveloped him like a shroud, the garment having been tossed over his head by the rather large man who had crashed into the foyer (after nearly breaking down the door with his imperious knocking), breathing fire. "Lady—Lady Penelope, sir?" the butler squeaked, blowing at a longish, errant lock of thinning hair which had fallen into his eyes. "Is that who you want?"

"I sure as blazes don't want that quoting widget Lucinda—'A word to the wise is enough,' she says. What words, I ask you? She gave me a hundred words, and I didn't understand a one of them. Now where's my daughter? What has that brainless booby done with her? *Penny!*" he shouted up at the wide stairway. "Papa's here, and eveything will be just fine!"

"Papa!" Cosmo shouted, racing down the stairs in his slippers after the sound of his father's voice had rudely blasted him from his bed, where he had been lying, trying to think of some way out of this dilemma. Still tying the sash around his midnight blue silk banyan, he exclaimed, "Thank heaven you've come—although I didn't think you'd be here so soon. I only just sent my letter. Or did you figure out where we had gone off to and follow us?"

"Follow you?" the Marquess repeated belligerently, grabbing onto Cosmo's left ear and pulling him toward the drawing room. "I'll give you 'follow you.' What do you think I am—a bloody puppy dog? I follow nobody. I knew where you and that useless brother of yours were heading the moment I discovered you missing. I wasn't chasing after you—it's Lucinda's ridiculous letter I'm here to find out about. Now, where's your sister? Lucinda said something about some knave sending sheep's eyes at Penny, and some drivel about playing with cats. Is your sister all right? I never should have tricked her into that wager.''

" 'I've heard old cunning stagers say fools for arguments use wagers,' Butler.''

"Lucinda!'' the Marquess ejaculated, whirling around to confront his cousin, who had somehow come up behind him without his hearing her. "Still dressing like a looby, ain't you? And wearing paint on your lips—at your age! Shame on you. What have you done with my daughter? Is she all right? She's in some sort of trouble, isn't she?''

" 'O most lame and impotent conclusion,' Shakespeare,'' Aunt Lucinda said admonishingly, wagging her head in the negative while secretly wishing she could bop her insulting relative on his overripe nose. Looby, indeed! She had never thought Philo Rayburn to be any great prize himself, him and his Greeks. Then, turning to Cyril, who had come to stand beside her, his arm wrapped protectively around her shoulders, she lamented sadly, " 'These are the effects of doting age—vain doubts, and idle cares, and over caution,' Dryden.''

"Aunt Lucinda believes Penny to be just fine, Papa,'' Cyril said quickly, stepping between his aunt and father before the latter could launch a rebuttal. "Cosmo and I aren't quite as sure, but we think she'll be all right.''

The Marquess looked from one son to the other, trying to decide whether or not he should take the time to murder them, then allowed himself to be led to a chair as Farnley showed signs of latent brilliance by slipping a full glass of burgundy into the man's hand.

"What's happened?'' the concerned father asked yet again, hoping he sounded in control of his emotions. "Your aunt sent me a letter hinting of trouble. It arrived the same day I woke to find you two hellions missing, and I came as soon as I could. Did Penny have an accident?''

"Yes,'' said Cosmo.

"No,'' said Cyril.

"Well, sort of,'' amended Cosmo, looking at his brother.

"Which is it?'' Philo asked, his expression furious.

"It's a little of both, actually,'' Cyril explained, jumping into the breech.

"Truth to tell, Papa," Cosmo went on, balancing from one bare foot to the other as the drawing room floor was rather cold, and he dared not move to the carpet or else put himself within ear-pinching reach of his father. "Penny did have a bit of a mishap on that brute Nemesis. Nothing too serious, you understand, but—"

"Boys! Will you get to the point!" the Marquess exploded, half rising to his feet. How he hated these twin conversations, with both of them saying so much while telling him so little. Besides, he was getting a crick in his neck from looking back and forth between them.

"She took a jump without looking first," Cyril concluded rapidly, believing it was best to start at the very beginning and work his way to their most unsettling news. "She wasn't hurt, but the man racing her got quite a bump on his head."

"Lost his memory for a space," Cosmo cut in, looking meaningfully at his brother as he silently warned him to stick to the story they had decided on earlier—the one that should keep their sister from becoming a widow before she ever became a wife. "He's Lucien Kenrick—Philippos's friend—the Earl of Leighton. He and Penny are betrothed."

The burgundy that had just entered the Marquess's parched mouth exited in a fine spray, dusting his waistcoat with a rash of small, reddish spots. *"Married! My Penelope?* To that bounder, Leighton? It's one thing for Philippos to run with him, but not my Penelope! Of all the men she could have chosen . . . Lucinda, you twit, how did you let such a terrible thing happen?"

Chapter Twelve

"DID YOU hear someone yelling just then, my lord? Oh drat it all, I wish I knew what I should discard. I never could abide whist. It's just too confusing."

Lucien sat at his ease across the width of the lacquered table from Lady Penelope in the sunlit morning room, his body turned to one side in the high-backed chair and his legs crossed negligently at the ankles, as he watched the way her smooth brow creased above her eyebrows while she concentrated on the game, pretending he did not feel the urge to lean across the tabletop and kiss the faint lines away.

They had been playing since immediately after breakfast, and had anyone other than the novice Lady Penelope been his opponent, he knew he would have lost half his fortune by now and been forced to put up the plain gold ring that glowed dully on his little finger. He just couldn't seem to keep his full concentration on the cards, distracted as he was by her early-morning beauty and offhand charm.

"Farnley has probably just come upon the broom I propped precariously against the pantry door, poor fellow," he explained obliquely in answer to her question as he reached forward to cover her reluctantly played card with his own. "Bad choice, my dear gamester. Obviously you haven't been paying attention. You should have known I was saving this."

Lady Penelope looked at the card the Earl had just played and threw down the remainder of her hand in disgust. "Oh, fudge! You've won again. I shall never get the straight of this game. I can now understand why you wished me to play; Papa would be outraged in the extreme to learn what a woefully inept card player I am. As it is,

I can't wait to see Cosmo's face when you tell him you want me to set up a faro bank in London once we're married. He'll soon be begging me to forget he ever brought up the silly idea of an engagement between us. Now, sir— as I shall not let you off so easily—I demand an explanation of your last vague statement. Why should Farnley have an attack of the vapors over a broom?"

Gathering up the scattered cards and beginning to dexterously shuffle them for the next hand, Lucien informed his student of a little prank he had played on the butler. He had propped a broom in such a way that it would fall directly into Farnley's path as he opened the pantry door. "According to a very interesting little book I found in your aunt's library this morning, it is considered to be quite a powerful ill omen, portending all sorts of simply dire misfortune. With any luck, Farnley shall barricade himself in his rooms for a sennight in order to outwit the curse. It was mean of me, of course—almost juvenile, in fact—but I think I deserve some recompense for having had that ferret pushing gruel down my gullet for two days."

Lady Penelope lightly covered her mouth with her hand to hide the smile his words provoked. "Be careful, my lord. You should put a halt to such deviltry, else you might just make me start liking you," she warned with forced solemnity. "Now tell me, how much do I owe you after that last rubber? It passes belief how dreadful I am at this game."

Lucien consulted the small paper that lay beside his left elbow as he busied himself in dealing out the cards. "I haven't added it yet, but I should say it's a little more than two thousand pounds; a mere pittance for a really dedicated gamester. I've seen more lost on a single turn of the cards at White's. We shall have to see that your father adds it to your dowry, won't we?"

"When billiard balls grow hair!" came an aggrieved roar from the doorway, causing Lucien's hand to hesitate momentarily in midair over the center of the table before continuing the deal.

"Your papa to the rescue, my dear. How fortuitous is his timing," Lucien whispered quickly out of the corner of his mouth, winking at Lady Penelope (who was, unfortunately, looking more guilty than gleeful) before he rose to his feet to greet the intruder, who was advancing on him with a decidedly militant look in his eyes.

"Good morning to you, sir," he began smoothly, holding out his right hand as he stopped in front of the large man, a welcoming smile on his handsome face. "You could only be the Marquess of Weybridge, my dearest Penny's father. How good of you to come. You're here to offer us your blessing, of course. And to allow me to make my offer in form, I hope, as this has been rather a ramble-shamble affair, hasn't it?"

"*Papa!*" Lady Penelope interrupted before her father could find his tongue (which may have been for the best, as his only daughter had yet to be exposed to the Marquess's admirable command of barracks language), catapulting herself into his arms and planting huge, smacking kisses on both of his cheeks as he held her against his chest in self-defense. "How wonderful it is to see you!"

"For the love of Zeus, Penny, calm yourself!" the Marquess pleaded in a choked voice, disengaging her clinging hands from around his abused throat. "Anyone would think we've been parted for years the way you're carrying on. Let me sit down and catch my breath."

So saying, the Marquess walked across the room to the card table and took up his daughter's chair, his hand going out to pick up and examine Lady Penelope's cards. "A little sleight of hand, Leighton?" he asked, shaking his head over the poor quality of cards his daughter had been dealt. "I didn't know you listed sharping among your talents—not that it surprises me, because it don't. For shame, sir."

Lady Penelope looked from one man to the other questioningly, then angrily. "He's been cheating?" she asked her father, incredulously. "You've been *cheating!*" she then accused the Earl, glaring at him. "Oh, how low can you be? Never mind. I know how low you can be. That's not fair! Why you dishonest, miserable—I understand now. It's no wonder I couldn't win!"

"Now, dearest," Lucien coaxed, holding his arms up in front of his face as if to avoid a physical attack, "be reasonable. How else were you to learn to watch out for cardsharps if I didn't teach you?''

Lady Penelope's eyes narrowed into angry slits. "Don't hand me that nonsense and expect me to swallow it whole. You were just toying with me. You never even told me what to look for, did you? Well, let me tell you, you can just go whistle for your two thousand pounds.''

"He can go whistle for your hand in marriage while he's at it,'' the Marquess slipped in with conviction. "I'll never give my approval to such a match. Cosmo must have put out his brain to let if he thinks I should do any such thing.''

If he had wished to gain the undivided attention of the other two occupants of the room, the Marquess had succeeded beyond his wildest imaginings with his last statement, for immediately two sets of eyes were staring at him, one pair opened wide in mingled shock and amazement, the other heavy-lidded and quietly considering.

"You refuse my offer, sir?'' the Earl said at last, the coolness in his voice alerting Lady Penelope to the sudden tenseness in the air. "Does this mean Philip will be prevailed upon to call me out? I shan't consider fighting you for—as much as I respect you, sir—I believe you are not an equal match for me in a duel, and I wouldn't wish to take advantage.''

"Philippos? A duel? Penny, what's the man talking about? There's no need for a duel. I've simply refused his suit, and that's the end of it.''

Lady Penelope rushed over to drop to the floor at her father's knees. "Of course there isn't, Papa,'' she assured him quickly, resting her hands on his beefy thigh as she looked up into his face. "I told Cosmo the whole thing was silly, but he said I was compromised and had to marry the Earl. I never knew Cosmo to be such a stickler for the proprieties. After all, it was only a kiss—two, actually, if you count last night when he had me drink the brandy, though I don't think that would be fair as I didn't quite know what I was doing at the time—and nothing to cause such drastic action as a betrothal.''

Lucien pressed his fingertips to his forehead, the Marquess's expression telling him that Cosmo may have said all this to Lady Penelope, but clearly, he had not been so forthcoming with his father. "Penny, my dear nodcock," he said in a resigned voice, "it would appear your father had not been totally brought up to date on our situation—a failing that, between us, we have just rectified, more's the pity."

"Papa," Cosmo began from the doorway (for he had felt he should be present for the interview that was taking place in the morning room and had finally eluded his aunt and brother long enough to join the small party), "I believe I should explain exactly—"

" 'Those who in quarrels interpose, must often wipe a bloody nose,' Gay," Aunt Lucinda prophesied quietly, entering the room to take hold of the well-meaning Cosmo by the elbow and urge him to withdraw.

Lady Penelope was left reeling in an effort to regain her balance as her father leapt to his feet to confront his second oldest son. "You didn't tell me Penny had been compromised by this grinning jackanapes—and why are you still in your dressing gown at this hour of the morning? Never mind that now. Cosmo, just five minutes ago you told me Penny was betrothed. You never said a thing about compromise. What's the matter, didn't you think it was important? Or did it just slip your mind? I swear, neither you nor Cyril ever got the straight of anything in your lives. Now we've either got to go along with the marriage or risk your brother Philippos in a duel to avenge Penny's honor."

Reaching down to help his fiancée to her feet, Lucien said silkily to the room at large, "I believe that does about sum it up, yes. But as I am so in love with my dearest Penny, I do hope you won't force me to spill friend Philip's claret all over some woodland glen in order to avenge her honor. I am more than happy to continue the engagement as it stands. Indeed, the only way I will agree to the dissolution of the betrothal would be if Lady Penelope cries off, which would also negate any more talk of duelling."

As he spoke, Lucien gave Lady Penelope's forearm a warning squeeze so that she would not immediately proclaim her willingness—nay, her eagerness—to cry off from the engagement, allowing all their plans to use the engagement to show how badly they suited each other to go for naught.

Unfortunately for Lucien (or so it would seem to the uninformed bystander, like Aunt Lucinda, who was already deeply involved in planning what she would wear to the wedding), the Marquess immediately responded in a very unfatherly way. "It doesn't matter a tinker's curse one way or the other what my daughter thinks."

"But, Papa—" Lady Penelope began, only to quickly close her mouth at the sight of the thundercloud expression on her father's face.

"It's either a duel or a marriage, Penny," the Marquess continued, "and as I have already refused the marriage, there is nothing else left to do—Philippos will challenge your so-called betrothed to a duel. I can see no other way to satisfy the Rayburn honor. Cosmo, go get dressed. I know where Philippos is staying, and I want you to ride over there directly with a message from me. I'll write it out, thank you, so that you can't forget any of the important parts. By the end of the week, we'll have this thing settled once and for all."

"You wish Philip to fight me, my lord?" Lucien asked, a small tic starting to work in his cheek. "I beg you to reconsider. I have no wish to duel with my best friend."

"Your wishes mean less than nothing to me, young man," the Marquess pointed out as he pushed Cosmo out of the room ahead of him. "Unless you wish to paint yourself a thorough coward and run off."

Lady Penelope sat down heavily in her chair after her father and brother had gone. "And you won't do that, will you?" she asked Lucien fatalistically. "Oh, no, you're too *honorable* to run away. That's how we got in this awful mess in the first place. Honorable? Hah! Honor from a man who invents imaginary wives and cheats defenseless young women at cards. Now you and Philippos are going to fight a duel. How did I ever get into this terrible predicament?"

Aunt Lucinda put a comforting arm around her niece's shoulders, pressing her rouged cheek against the top of the reddish gold head. " 'We have seen better days,'

Shakespeare," she agreed mournfully, wondering worriedly if the pattern she had chosen from *La Belle Assemblée* would make up tolerably well in funereal black.

"It's all *his* fault," Lady Penelope declared, glaring at Lucien as she sniffed back her tears.

Aunt Lucinda seemed to agree, saying feelingly, " 'If I can catch him once upon the hip, I will feed fat the ancient grudge I bear him,'—"

"Will Shakespeare," Leighton supplied, adjusting his already perfect cravat with one lean hand. "I can see how I am to be cast as the villain in this piece. However, I should like you ladies to remember something Syrus said: 'It matters not what you are thought to be, but what you are.' Think of me what you will, I must serve my own twisted notion of propriety. I could never forgive myself if I slid my tail between my legs and slunk off rather than stayed and faced Philip. And now, ladies, if you will excuse me, I believe I will leave you for a space. I have much to think about, and I have found I tend to do that best on horseback."

Three hours later, after running Hades up and down every field within the space of three miles, Lucien at last sat with his back against the trunk of an old apple tree at the crest of a small hill near the estate, absently shredding a dried leaf in his hands as he tried to sort out his muddled thoughts which no amount of racing aboard his spirited stallion had yet been able to align into any workable plan of action.

Nothing was going according to plan—as nothing had since he'd first espied Lady Penelope Rayburn flying on her grey gelding across the same empty field now spread out below him, her glorious hair streaming behind her like fingers of living fire in the breeze.

He'd really thought their bizarre little plan was working—Cosmo and Cyril certainly seemed to have been having second thoughts about the wisdom of the betrothal after seeing their beloved sister much the worse for demon drink last night—but he hadn't planned on the Marquess's showing up today to voice his opposition to the match.

In truth, he had been confident the twins would have

given him his marching orders within a few more days, before the Marquess could reach Wormhill, and the whole unfortunate comedy of errors would have been over. He would then have been free to examine his real feelings at some distance from Lady Penelope, before casually running into her during the coming Season. By that time he might have decided that she was nothing more than another comely young beauty and not the single creature in the world to ever capture his entire heart. But it hadn't worked out that way, and the Marquess's opposition had opened up an entirely new set of problems Leighton hadn't even considered.

After all, from the way Lady Penelope had spoken (complained, actually, but now was not the time to be splitting hairs), it would seem that it was the man's greatest wish to have his daughter married off, and an Earl should suit him right down to the ground. Yes, the Marquess's vehement objection to the betrothal was confusing, to say the least.

Lucien opened his hands and allowed the remnants of the leaf to sift through his fingers and float down onto the ground between his bent knees, cursing himself for refusing to allow the engagement to be dissolved unless Lady Penelope herself insisted upon it. At the time, he had not wished to give the lie to their original plan of making everyone believe the two of them were genuinely in love— the ploy had seemed to be working nicely enough—but as it had fallen out, that now appeared to be his biggest miscalculation to date.

It headed a long list of miscalculations, the very worst of those being that he hadn't planned on tumbling into love with Lady Penelope Rayburn, for—unless he was very wrong—he had somehow done just that. "Damn!" he swore out loud, pulling up a clump of wilting grass and flinging it into the slight wind, where the blades danced about for a moment before seeking refuge on the toes of his highly polished Hessians. "Damn and blast! You're a thousand times a fool, Leighton, old sport, and you deserve everything you're about to get!"

"I came up here to give you a piece of my mind, but even I don't believe I can improve upon that statement,"

Lady Penelope declared passionately, dropping to her knees beside him on the damp grass, clad once more in her fetching midnight blue riding outfit and trailing Nemesis's reins in one gloved hand. "But if you're heaping abuse on your own head, please don't allow your hopes to be raised by waiting for me to stop you, for I have a rather vested interest in seeing you laid low."

Lucien, his elbows still resting on his knees, turned to look inquiringly at his companion. "I didn't hear you ride up," he said inanely (at least from his point of view), but then he told himself he hadn't said anything particularly quotable in quite some time. "Outrun your groom again? You're a naughty piece, although I don't blame you. I shouldn't like a shadow behind me everywhere I went.

"Tell me, has your father sent off a note to Philip at Crompton's? I imagine he could be here by nightfall, if he leaves at once, or tomorrow morning at the latest. Let us pray he doesn't feel it necessary to bring dearest Lady Redfern and her nubile daughter Dorinda along to watch the fun, as I don't think even I deserve that much punishment. My lady, may I wear your favor on my sleeve as I go into combat? Or perhaps you'd rather sling one of your scarves across my chest. It might then make a good target for your brother's pistol."

Lady Penelope sat down with a dull thud, allowing Nemesis's reins to trail on the ground, as she had trained him too well to worry about the horse wandering very far away. "You men, you're all so bloodthirsty! I can't believe you'd actually fight a duel over me. It's so—so *archaic*. And why did you say all that drivel about me having to be the one to cry off? Most especially that ridiculous farra-diddle about loving me? You know it's all a hum. Why, I can't imagine a single thing that would serve to make you more ecstatic than to be waving farewell to me as you ride out of my life."

Lucien tipped his head and looked across at her, his smile a trifle lopsided—and rather sad. "Yes, I have given you that impression, haven't I? When I haven't been busy compromising you, that is."

Hastily picking up a small handful of leaves, Lady Penelope made herself busy arranging them into a small fan, keeping her face averted until the hot rush of color that had invaded her cheeks at his last words had time to fade. "I'd rather not discuss that particular part of our association, if you don't mind. There's nothing we can do to alter the past. Frankly, it's the future I'm worried about."

Lucien leaned back against the tree trunk once again, gazing up at the thin November sun through the thick mass of tangled branches. "I believe we can safely drop our plan to show how extremely well we two pranksters should suit," he reasoned aloud. "I do find that a bit of a let-down, truth to tell, for I had already half planned to shock your brothers with a duet tonight after dinner—a slightly risqué drinking song I was going to teach you this after-noon. Pity."

Lady Penelope nodded in solemn agreement, for she had rather enjoyed her small lessons in drinking and gam-bling, although she had pretended a slight loss of memory herself this morning over breakfast concerning most of what had taken place after she had drunk the brandy the previous evening. "Can't you still teach me the song?" she asked wistfully. "I promise not to sing it in polite company once I am forced to go to London for the Season. I don't think Papa has had time to think of it yet, but he is sure to realize quite soon that he has won our wager."

She was sitting so close to the Earl that she could feel his shoulders shake as he gave a rueful chuckle at her innocent question. Yes, she would have liked shocking her brothers with the song, almost as much as she was sure he would have enjoyed teaching it to her.

They really did suit very well, she thought, even if they had only set out to pretend as much to frighten Cosmo into abandoning his determination to have them betrothed. In fact, it was amazing exactly how well suited they were.

They shared the same strange (or at least her Papa cer-tainly would say so) sense of humor, and she had already discovered that they both held many of the same interests. As a matter of fact, she realized with a start, if Philippos had brought Lucien to Weybridge Manor when she was younger, she probably would have developed a ridiculous, girlish crush on him and driven him crazy with her attentions, following him about everywhere as she had done with her oldest brother.

But she hadn't met him and had instead grown up deciding that she loved Weybridge more than she could ever love any man. She had determined never to marry, never to leave her beloved home, never to allow any man to rule her.

Would Leighton have tried to rule her in the way of the usual English marriage? she wondered, stealing a look at him from beneath her lashes. Would he have forced her into the role of well-behaved society matron and stifled her every urge to be herself—free and unfettered?

No, she decided, he wouldn't. He would treat her as an equal, a co-conspirator in his plan to enjoy life to the fullest and the devil take the hindmost. They could have had a wonderful life together: laughing, and loving, and raising a gaggle of extremely independent children who would be the light of their hearts and the scourge of the countryside.

Lady Penelope felt the sting of tears behind her eyes as she purposefully banished such self-defeating thoughts to the back of her brain. This was no time for useless daydreaming. They had a real problem on their hands.

"You really will fight Philippos?" she asked at last, biting her bottom lip. "I don't understand. I thought you two were friends?"

"We are friends," Lucien answered quietly, "and, no, I won't fight him. I can't."

Lady Penelope didn't know whether to be happy or sad. "Then you've changed your mind? You'll leave before Philippos can get here to challenge you?"

Lucien shook his head. "I can't do that either, Penny," he told her, reaching over to take the hand she had involuntarily held out to him, as if she didn't want him to go even as she urged him to leave. "Please understand, a gentleman has a certain sense of honor—"

"Honor! How I am learning to hate that word! Where is the honor in dying? Oh, Lucien," she pleaded, squeezing his hand tightly as she leaned toward him in her anxiety, "I don't think I could bear it if—if—"

"If Philip should be hurt," Lucien completed for her as her voice trailed off.

She looked at him for a few moments longer before lowering her head. "Yes—yes, of course—if Philippos should be hurt."

"He won't be, I guarantee it," Lucien promised, releasing her hand as he rose to his feet.

"How can you guarantee such a thing?" Lady Penelope asked as he reached down to help her to rise. "You'll both have pistols."

Lucien didn't answer her until he had helped her to mount Nemesis and untied Hades's reins from the tree. "It doesn't matter, my dearest Penny," he told her just before he slapped his hand to Nemesis's rump and sent the gelding pelting off down the hillside so that she couldn't hear his last words. "You see, I plan to delope."

Chapter Thirteen

THE MARQUESS was alone in the darkened morning room, his hands stuck deep in his pockets and his heavily jowled chin denting his cravat as he sat slumped in an uncomfortable chair (he had begun to believe there did not exist a single comfortable chair in the entirety of Wormhill and had actually been appalled at the sight of Jerome Benedict's monstrosities in the drawing room; no Greek could have conceived of such ugliness), trying to understand how he had been brought to this pass.

All he had wanted to do was marry off his daughter. Was that so bad? Was his wish so terrible that he should be punished in this way? So he had made a silly wager, knowing full well he had stacked the odds entirely in his favor by including the silly Lucinda Benedict in his plans. It was an inspired plan, one which should have succeeded beyond his wildest dreams. How was he to know Lucien Kenrick was going to show up and destroy everything?

Earlier in the afternoon Cyril had filled him in on all the particulars of what had transpired since his daughter had arrived in Wormhill, and it did not make for a pretty story. Lady Penelope had clearly lost the wager—for she had got herself into a scrape just as her father had hoped she would (and in even less time than he had predicted)—but Philo Rayburn had certainly never planned on the child allowing herself to be compromised.

And by Lucien Kenrick, no less! the Marquess thought, wincing. Leave it to Penny to stumble upon the most unsuitable man in all of England and then become betrothed to him within the week—she who had vowed never to marry! The whole situation was beyond comprehension. If it had been any other man, perhaps he would have allowed it, he thought (for he was a desperate man and should be forgiven his little wishes), but the Earl of Leighton was totally out of the running in Philo's list of prospective bridegrooms.

Now to make matters even worse, his own family was turning against him.

Lucinda, whose opinions he may not have valued, but a lady difficult to ignore, had wagged her finger in his face as he had taken her arm to lead her in to dinner and declared, " 'He that will keep a monkey should pay for the glasses he breaks,' Selden,'' a sentiment with which the Marquess certainly had to agree, although he did not understand why she had said it. She had then shaken off his hand and refused to speak to him again, which was perhaps the only high spot in his visit thus far.

His younger sons, Cosmo and Cyril, had begged an audience with him before Cosmo set out to Crompton's, persecuting him with their inane back and forth comments and half-completed sentences which had a great deal to do with Lucien Kenrick being a ''right good sport, all things considered, seeing as how we did tie him up,'' and Penny seeming to ''like the fella well enough; or at least better than anyone else she's ever seen.''

His only daughter and the light of his life—who had, after all, been the one compromised, and who should be thrilled that he had begun plans to avenge her honor—had fled from the morning room in tears not a half hour ago, loudly lamenting that she was sure that either Philippos or Leighton was going to be killed before warning, ''It will *all* be on your head, Papa, and I shall never forgive you!''

Lady Penelope's visit had come just before that of her brother Philippos—the exhausted Earl of Hawkedon had arrived just before midnight, looking more cherub than avenging angel—who had proceeded to read his father a homily on friendship (during which he utterly refused to challenge this same Leighton), and then stomped out of the room in high dudgeon after declaring, ''They'll be building snowmen in Hades before I'll lift my hand against Lucien—even if he did stick me in bed with a blinking salmon!''

All in all, the Marquess was feeling very much abused.

He did have one ally—a rather sad looking shrimp he'd heard Cyril address as Farnley—but as the fellow had stopped him in the hallway after dinner to press a large hagstone into his hand to ward off demons (before slinking back to the kitchens, peering fearfully over his shoulder all the way), Philo wasn't much comforted by Farnley's expression of approval.

A slight rapping at the door caught his attention, and he bellowed "go away," wishing to be left alone in his misery. The rapping stopped, but his head came up abruptly as he heard the latch lifting just before the door opened to show the Earl of Leighton silhouetted against the light from the hallway. "If I had known it was you, I wouldn't have wasted my breath. You never were one to take no for an answer, were you?"

Lucien advanced into the room, taking up the straight-backed chair he had sat on earlier while playing cards with Lady Penelope and turning it around so he could straddle it, facing the Marquess. "It's funny you should say something leading like that, sir, for I was in a quandary as to how to bring up the subject. You see, a question has been nagging at me all day. I've never met you before, and although you have every reason to hate me for playing fast and loose with your daughter, I get the feeling your dislike stems from quite another source. Am I correct?"

Philo looked at Lucien from beneath lowered eyelids, liking the way the younger man came to the point. At least he wasn't wishy-washy. His profile is even the least bit Greek, he thought, admiring the Earl's straight, high-bridged nose. "You've got a bit of a reputation as a hell-raiser, son," he said, weighing his words carefully, "even if Wellington mentioned you in his dispatches more than once. You don't seem to approach life with the seriousness it deserves. It makes a man wonder if you've any proper notion of responsibility. After all, you're as old as Philippos, yet you're still racketing about the countryside like you was still in your salad days."

"I shall not defend myself to you on that score, for I admit to enjoying my life, but I do know where my responsibilities lie. As a matter of fact, I seem to be doing a lot of explaining lately concerning my responsibilities with you Rayburns, and I believe I'm getting used to it. I've just come back into Society after spending nearly a year running my father's estates during his illness. No," Lucien went on consideringly, "I think there is much more to it than that. After all, Philip lives much as I do. None of us has been in much of a hurry to settle down after spending so many months away in the war. Rather making up for lost time, I think is what we have all been about."

"Yes, well . . ." Philo put in slowly, searching for something else to say that would keep him from saying what he knew he must.

"I still fail to see why my rackety ways should make me an unfit husband, sir," Lucien cut in when it seemed the Marquess was going to rise. "I have a ridiculously ample fortune of my own, besides my allowance and my expectations. I have a town house in London and two estates that have come down to me through my mother. I'm young, healthy, and fairly well liked within my circle. Although my betrothal to Penny came about in a rather shabby fashion, I cannot see why you insist on settling things on the field of honor. If you cannot like me as a son-in-law, why not just allow your daughter to cry off? I can see no reason why the story of her compromise should ever leave these walls. And, truth to tell, I don't think Penny's heart would be broken."

"And yours?" Philo asked, rising to his feet to look down closely at the Earl as he spoke. "Are your emotions involved? I have heard all that transpired—including that ridiculousness about you being a married man—and I am not so blockheaded as to believe that you were in favor of this betrothal. Or have you had a change of heart?"

"My feelings don't enter into it, sir," Lucien pointed out repressively, also rising, so that he stood eye to eye with the Marquess. "And you still haven't answered my question. Why are you so adamant about this duel?"

"I had hoped to finish this business without having to refer to this sordidness, but you force my hand. Very well, Leighton, my late wife was second cousin to Caspar McCulloch, poor man," the Marquess announced baldly, watching as Lucien flinched. "Although the Marchioness died soon after Penny was born, I still keep in touch with her side of the family. The scandal may never have left Aberfoyle, but I know how you destroyed his only daughter, Ann Louise."

The Earl remained stock-still, his complexion ghastly white as he stared at the Marquess, unblinking. "If you say so, sir," he returned at last in a dull, defeated voice.

"I don't have to say so. Caspar wrote me all about it. He's had a seizure in this past year, you know, not that it surprises me. He's never been the same since his daughter's death. Now," Philo finished wearily, "will you please allow me to pass? Four o'clock comes early, and you and I have an appointment in the clearing behind the stables. We'll dispense with seconds, as I should like to have this matter settled before my family can get wind of it and try to interfere."

Lucien was in shock. His broad shoulders slumped forward in defeat, and it wasn't until the Marquess had reached the door that he realized all that the man had said. "You, sir? I thought I was to face Philip."

Philo drew himself up to his full height and turned to face the younger man. "In truth, this quarrel is nearly fifteen years old and of no real concern to my son—or my daughter. If I had not known your history, I probably would have welcomed you into my family with open arms, for settling Penelope satisfactorily will be a problem, and I think she likes you well enough, more's the pity. But I do know your history, sir, and I am not prepared to allow you to repeat it with my daughter. Now, good night to you, sir, until we meet tomorrow. I understand you are quite good with pistols, and I shall have the pair I keep in my traveling coach prepared for your inspection. Please be prompt."

Lucien stayed in the morning room for another hour, alone with his thoughts.

Ann Louise had reached out of the grave to snatch at his chance for happiness.

Ann Louise. His wife.

His life had come full circle.

It was time to pay the piper.

The level of cherry brandy in the cut glass decanter

beside his elbow continued to fall as the Earl contemplated the twisted workings of Fate. He had been so young—even younger than Lady Penelope was now—when he had traveled north to Scotland to visit the sights.

With France still in an uproar, the Continent was not safe for touring, his father had warned, never knowing the trouble his eldest son would encounter just outside the small village of Aberfoyle.

Lucien had met Ann Louise McCulloch quite by accident while out riding one day—much as he had met Lady Penelope—and had been immediately captivated by her wild, dark beauty.

She was just seventeen, barely out of the schoolroom, and he had fallen in love with all the passionate intensity of the very young. They met many times over the next two weeks, keeping their rendezvous a secret between them, as Ann Louise had told him she was not yet willing to share their love with the world. Lucien agreed, as he had agreed with everything this bewitching creature had to say.

So smitten was he with her that he at last approached her father for her hand in marriage, only to be told Ann Louise had been betrothed since birth to a solid member of the local gentry who had been away visiting his Jamaican estates for the past three years. Lucien's heart was broken, and he had raced across the open countryside like a madman before drinking himself into oblivion in the shrubbery outside her bedroom window.

When he awoke it was to the darkness that settled over the land just before dawn, his muddled brain reeling with the knowledge that his beloved lay sleeping just beyond his reach. He remembered their last, tearful meeting behind the dairy, during which Ann Louise had talked wildly of eloping, telling him that it seemed the only answer to their problems. She hated her fiancé, he was old—all of forty—and smelled bad into the bargain. She had sobbed on Lucien's shoulder, brokenhearted, begging for him to help her.

Before he could stop to think, before the sun could rise, he had climbed the rough stone wall to her chamber and spirited her away to the nearest blacksmith, and they had declared their vows over the anvil. It wasn't the ceremony

Lucien would have chosen, but Ann Louise had sworn to him that it was binding, and her father would have no choice but to allow them to be married again in the kirk.

Ann Louise had refused to retire to a nearby inn with her new husband, but insisted instead on returning to her father's house to tell him what they had done. The irate McCulloch had immediately turned Lucien over to his four brawny sons, who had left him in no condition to assert his husbandly rights for several weeks, while his dearest wife carefully avoided his sickroom because the sight of his battered and bruised face upset her tender sensibilities.

Lucien took another deep drink of his brandy as he remembered the night he at last was free to visit his wife in her adjoining chamber. When he had entered the room, Ann Louise had been sitting at her dressing table, pulling a brush through her long black hair, her lush young body clearly visible through her sheer nightdress. He had stood like a man transfixed, scarcely able to believe his luck. She had been worth all the pain, worth every moment he had spent longing for her, and now he would at last be free to hold her in his arms and love her as he had longed to do.

She had appeared startled at his appearance, trying in vain to cover her body with her hands as she ordered him to leave her, and then had run from his passionate embrace when he tried to kiss her, dashing out into the hallway and racing for the stairway as he watched, dumbfounded, from the doorway.

"And then, as I called after her, begging my beloved wife to come back to me—her adoring husband who had willingly suffered much in her sweet name—she tripped over the hem of her gown and plummeted down the stairs," Lucien said out loud in a dull voice, staring into the darkness that had enveloped the morning room as the last candle sputtered and died.

Ann Louise hadn't died in the fall, but had lingered for three days after losing the baby she had been carrying. Without ever regaining consciousness, she had simply faded away. McCulloch and his sons had been devastated and laid all the blame at Lucien's door, assuaging their grief by once again beating the young Earl into a jelly before taking him deep into the wild countryside and leaving him to die.

Lucien hadn't attended the funeral, which had taken place while he was still recovering in a crofter's loft many miles from Aberfoyle. He never learned if there had been a man in attendance who was mourning his lost love, his lost child, but he assumed that there was—and assumed the man was married to another. The thoroughly disillusioned young Earl had only concentrated on regaining his health and returning to England, where he hoped he could one day forget that Ann Louise McCulloch had ever existed.

That love had ever existed.

That trust had ever existed.

And he had forgotten, for nearly fifteen years—until he had been out on yet another solitary ride and encountered yet another beautiful young girl, and fallen in love once more.

But his long-ago lesson had taught him to mistrust more than females in general; he had also learned to mistrust his own judgement.

That was why he had fought his attraction to Lady Penelope from the very first. That was why he had hoped to dissolve the betrothal—so that he could put some time and space between them until he could better measure the feelings in his heart.

That was also why, now that he knew beyond a doubt that he loved Lady Penelope Rayburn with every drop of blood that was in him, he also knew that in just a few short hours he would be spilling that blood as her father blew a small, deadly hole in the center of his chest.

For, although he had been Ann Louise's victim, he could not destroy her memory to her father by telling Philo the truth now, nearly fifteen years later. He had made that decision long ago, and would not change it.

His only regret was that his dearest Penny would never know how much he loved her, how she had come breezing into his life and forced him to search beneath the façade of joviality that he wore, to rediscover the love and tenderness he had thought gone forever.

"Congratulations, Lucien," he told himself, downing

the last of the brandy before rising to quit the room. "To-day, at long last, you are a man. I wonder if Lucinda Benedict ever heard of Suetonius, the wise man who wrote, 'We who are about to die salute you'?''

Lucien had returned to his room only to splash water on his face and seek out a fresh change of linen before meeting the Marquess. He did not go near the high bed until he had stripped off his jacket and sought out a seat in order to pull off his Hessians, which explained why he had not at once noticed the slight mound that appeared beneath the coverlet.

Once he had, however, he instinctively knew that Philip had not been waiting in his rooms to speak to him about arranging a time and place for their duel, then retired to the bed when he had grown weary. No, this was a very different visitor, with a very different reason for being there.

Crossing the room to take up the small candle he had brought upstairs with him, Lucien retraced his steps to hold the light over the bed so that he could get a clear picture of Lady Penelope Rayburn as she slept. The dark sweep of her lashes shadowed her pale cheeks, and he smiled in spite of himself as he saw that her full lips pouted most delightfully even in sleep. Her shoulders were bare, he had noticed immediately, her heavy, unbound hair caressing her clear white skin as it tumbled about her head. She was beautiful in her slumber; young, virginal, and infinitely appealing.

And she was in his bed, waiting for him.

Why? his tortured brain asked as he clenched his left hand into a tight fist. What is she trying to tell me? Dear God, is she sacrificing her body in the hope I won't blow a hole in her brother? Has my life come to this—that I should spend my last night on this earth wrapped in the arms of someone who will pretend to love me in order to save another? Am I to be left nothing, not even my pride?

Lucien set down the brass candle holder with a loud thump, deliberately waking his uninvited guest. Her emerald green eyes shot wide open at once, instantly clear, instantly alert, and she pulled the coverlet up over her breasts as she turned onto her back and looked up at him.

"I must have fallen asleep," she said, pushing herself into a sitting position against the headboard, wetting her lips. Something in Lucien's eyes told her that he was angry. He was very angry. She had expected many things from him once he discovered her lying here, but she hadn't expected him to be angry. "I've been waiting for you."

Lucien ran his gaze assessingly down the length of the bed to the point where her small feet (her toes tightly curled in apprehension and just a bit of embarrassment) made a small pyramid beneath the coverlet, and then slowly allowed his gaze to run back up her body, to concentrate on her flushed face. "Obviously," he said insolently, slowly beginning to unbutton his shirt. "If I promise to make it worth the wait, do you think you can possibly forgive me?"

Lady Penelope's eyes grew as wide as saucers while she watched him shrug out of his shirt, exposing his muscled chest. "What—what do you think you're doing now?" she gasped, pulling the coverlet high against her throat. "Surely you're not suggesting—"

"I'm not?" Lucien asked, holding his shirt away from him with one hand before opening his fingers and allowing it to drop into a small, provocative puddle of gleaming white silk atop the dark coverlet. "Why not?"

Suddenly Lady Penelope was angry. Very angry. She was at least as angry as he had been a moment earlier. "You know perfectly well why not! I came in here so that we could show Papa how thoroughly compromised I am, forcing him to give his blessing to our marriage. I heard you when you said you're planning to delope when you face Philippos, and I'm not so silly that I don't know what that means. Philippos could kill you. I know you never wanted this betrothal, but surely being married to me is less fatal than a bullet?"

Lucien sat down on the side of the bed in bewilderment. Once again he had misjudged her. She wasn't thinking of Philip; she was thinking of him, worrying about him, willing to sacrifice herself for him. She could have simply gone to her brother and told him about her betrothed's plan to delope, but she hadn't. She had chosen to involve herself personally. It boggled the mind! "Let me see if I understand this, Penny," he began slowly, hope beginning to grow deep in his heart. "You came in here tonight, stripped yourself down to the buff—"

"Please!" she interrupted, shocked in spite of herself to hear the words spoken aloud.

"—and climbed into my bed," he continued, bowing his head slightly in her direction, "in order that your father could discover us together in a compromising situation— I'll assume for argument's sake that your resident dragon, Doreen, is somewhere about, ready to sound the alarm at the appropriate moment—all to save me from a bullet?"

Lady Penelope nodded vigorously, thankful that he wasn't too much the worse for drink to understand. "Yes, yes. It's really quite elementary, but it's all I could think of on such short notice."

"Which probably explains why it has not yet occurred to you that if *I* am married to you, *you* are then married to me," Lucien remarked, reaching behind him to locate his shirt. "Or hasn't that fact as yet registered in your brain?"

"You could divorce me, I suppose . . . after a time," she said in a small voice, lowering her head so that her hair surrounded her face like a curtain.

Lucien threw back his head and laughed aloud in genuine amusement. "Oh, that's wonderful, it really is. Divorce you? Then your father would have me horsewhipped for a cad before he had Philip put a period to my existence. No, if we were to be married, my pet, we would have to stay married. Until we were both very old and very grey."

Lady Penelope flung back her head, sending her curls flying, and stuck out her chin in defiance. "And would that be so bad? Am I that awful that you'd rather die than live with me? Well, let me tell you, I hope Philippos blows two holes in you, for I think I hate you that much."

"Or love me that much," Lucien said quietly, seeing the tears that threatened to escape her liquid green eyes and run down her cheeks. "Which is it, sweetings? I really do need to know. You'll probably never know how much I need to hear you say you love me.''

It was very quiet in the room for several seconds, seconds during which Lucien Kenrick thought he could feel every beat of his heart measuring out the time as it pushed inexorably toward the hour of four. At last, Lady Penelope smiled and held out her bare arms in order to draw him close, allowing the coverlet to fall away without a single hint of shame or regret. ''I think you already know the answer to that question, Lucien. I love you. I love you very, very much.''

''Oh, Penny,'' he rasped, releasing his pent up breath. ''I truly don't deserve you, darling girl, but I do love you so. I love you with my very life.''

And then, his hands trembling, tears standing brightly in his eyes, Lucien cast the last of his fears behind him and reached out to love.

''*One . . . two . . . ,*''

Lucien and Philo counted out loud together as they began walking away from each other, their steps measured and slow as they held their pistols with the barrels raised, pointed toward the slowly brightening sky.

Lady Penelope had been sleeping when Lucien left her, stealing away silently without a single look back, or else his courage would have deserted him entirely.

''*three . . . four . . . ,*''

Farnley stood to one side, his knees shaking like dry bones in a sack as he held the empty dueling case in one hand and three rabbit's feet in the other, his eyes closed tight against the sight of blood.

It had almost gone six before everything could be arranged and the nearby doctor summoned to administer to the injured, and the sun was just coming up over the horizon as the two men walked on through the rising mist, their faces set and expressionless.

''*five . . . six . . . ,*''

Philo Rayburn knew he hadn't fought a duel since his grass time—and that had ended with he and his rival for Madamoiselle De Barge's favors going off arm in arm to a local tavern after both of them (much the worse for wine) had failed to shoot anything more vital than a tree limb and the left earlobe of Philo's second—and he was feeling every one of his three and sixty years.

He hadn't liked the look in Leighton's eyes, he remembered as he counted out the steps. The boy looked as if he had already become reconciled to dying. He didn't act at all like the rotter Caspar had described him as being: a heartless, soulless villain who despoiled young girls who would rather throw themselves down the stairs to their deaths than suffer his advances again.

Perhaps Caspar had been wrong. Perhaps he, too, was wrong to have believed the ravings of a shattered, grieving man. Perhaps his sons were right; perhaps Lucien Kenrick was a good man, an honorable man, a man he could give his daughter to with an easy heart.

"seven . . . eight . . . ,"

How he loved her, Lucien thought, staring at the bare trees and remembering the way Lady Penelope had fit into his arms, the way her head had nestled just so into the curve of his shoulder, her fiery curls burning into his bare skin. He could not in good conscience take all that she had offered so innocently, so willingly, but he had taken as much as he dared, which was only enough to make him regret he couldn't have fifty years more of loving her before he died.

The Marquess didn't know it, but he had a lot to be grateful for this morning. At least he wouldn't have to worry about marrying his daughter off to some local squire's son within the next few months in order to explain away Lucien's child.

A child, the Earl thought, almost missing a step in the count. He would have liked to have had a child with Penelope . . . several children . . . all with her glorious red-gold hair . . . and those wonderful emerald eyes . . . .

"nine . . . ten . . . ,"

The two men stopped, turned smartly on their heels, and extended their right arms toward each other, weapons cocked and at the ready. Farnley dropped the dueling case on his foot and quickly stuffed two of the furry rabbit's feet into his ears to block out the bark of the pistols.

Lady Penelope, who had been tossing restlessly ever

since Lucien's warmth had been removed from her back, did not have the butler's advantage of forewarning and therefore heard the shots quite clearly as they echoed loudly in the quiet morning air.

She immediately sat bolt upright and began to scream.

Chapter Fourteen

DOREEN Sweeney woke with a start, one hand immediately going up to rub the side of her neck, which had been forced into an extremely uncomfortable position when she had fallen asleep in the curtained alcove, her legs drawn up under her and her upper body propped sideways against the wall.

After pushing back the curtain, she shook her head for a moment to clear it before readjusting her nightcap, which had fallen forward over her eyes, struggling to understand how it had become light in the hallway when the last thing she could remember was the clock striking the hour of three.

"Blessed Mary!" she whispered, horrified. "It's listenin' I was supposed to be, for Lady Penelope's signal. They was talkin' for so long that I—Oh, for shame, Doreen, *what have you done?*"

Then she heard it again, the sound that had served to bring her awake. Lady Penelope was screaming!

"I'll make the rotter smell hell for that!" she vowed fervently, jumping to her feet in one quick motion and throwing open the heavy door to the Earl's chamber so that it smashed loudly against the wall.

"Oh, Doreen, thank heaven you're here," Lady Penelope called gratefully from behind the velvet curtains that hung around the bed. "You've got to help me!"

"*Arragh!* Get away from her, you spawn of the devil, or I'll make you scratch where you don't itch!" Doreen shouted, advancing into the room to throw back the velvet curtains with both hands, only to stop in confusion as she saw her mistress was quite alone. "Where'd he skelp off to, the bounder? I heard you screamin'. I must have nod-

173

ded off for a moment—ah, Missy, don't cry so. There, there, Doreen's here now and everythin's going to be just ducky.''

The maid gathered her charge into her comforting arms, aware that the child hadn't a stitch of clothes on her, *tsk-tsking* all the while as she searched in her robe for a handkerchief with which to wipe Lady Penelope's streaming eyes.

"He's gone and done it anyway, Doreen," Lady Penelope wailed, holding onto the maid convulsively as she tried to catch her breath. "Lucien and Philippos have fought a duel. I heard the shots just now. Oh, please, please, hurry and fetch me a gown. I have to go to him!"

The maid scurried out of the room only to return a few moments later with a hastily gathered ensemble that Lady Penelope fairly dove into, not bothering about either stockings or shoes or even the brush Doreen tried to pull through the tangled curls that tumbled onto her mistress's shoulders. In less than three minutes, the frantic Lady Penelope was in the hallway, racing toward the stairs, only to be halted by Philippos's outstretched arms.

"Philippos!" she exploded, realizing her eldest brother was still clad in his dressing gown. "What are you doing here? I heard shots, I'm sure of it. I thought you and Lucien had fought the duel anyway, even after we—never mind! I don't understand. What's happening? Where is everybody? Oh, let me go, I have to find Lucien."

"I told Papa last night I wouldn't have any part of dueling with my best friend. I thought he told you," Philippos explained quickly, motioning for Cosmo and Cyril, who had just stuck their heads out of their bedroom door, Cyril still wearing his tasseled nightcap, to join him in the hallway. "Here are the twins now. Boys, go see if Papa is in his room."

"I'd rather not, actually, if you want to know the truth. You go, Cosmo," Cyril urged quickly, stepping back a pace. "The last time I burst in on Papa when he was sound asleep, he threw a candlestick at me. Go on, you know he's always liked you best."

Just then another door opened, and Lucinda Benedict wandered into the hallway, clutching a trembling Pansy by the shoulders (Pansy, who had awakened earlier to discover that her beloved Farnley had somehow disappeared, had at once come racing to Aunt Lucinda for assistance, showing yet again that the Benedict butler's wife was none too bright).

The older woman held the slighter form of the weeping housekeeper in front of her in order to protect her modesty, the two of them therefore advancing down the hallway, matching step for step, in a curious, ducklike waddle. " 'Their rising all at once was as the sound of thunder heard remote,' Milton," Aunt Lucinda complained, obviously not well pleased to have been awakened so early.

"Oh, Aunt Lucinda," Lady Penelope lamented as she struggled to be free of her brother's restraining hands, "Lucien has fought a duel, I'm sure of it. I heard the shots. Tell Philippos I have to go to him."

"Papa's not in his rooms," Cosmo reported, rejoining the group, which now included two under-housemaids who had been in the process of opening the draperies farther down the hall and had been drawn by all the commotion. "I could be wrong, but I'll bet the old boy stole a march on you, Philippos, and faced Lucien himself. I wish he would have told us—it must have been quite a sight."

"Papa!" Lady Penelope shrieked. "Papa and Lucien? Philippos, do you really think—"

Pansy nodded furiously, stepping away from her mistress to address the gathering at large. "Farnley told me there'd be a shootin'. My Farnley's *so smart*. He's always right, yes, he is."

Aunt Lucinda's derisive sniff caught the housekeeper's attention, and she turned to look at the older woman, who was vainly trying to hide her draped form behind a nearby marble pedestal displaying a libelous bust of Julius Caesar with a cravat tied around his neck. " 'A fool must now and then be right by chance,' Cowper," Aunt Lucinda reminded them all, just as Lady Penelope at last succeeded in breaking away from her brother and ran toward the staircase.

She was just about at the bottom of the steps when the front door opened, admitting a dusty stream of early morning sunlight—as well as a perfectly healthy Lucien

Kenrick and her smiling father, who proceeded to saunter into the foyer arm in arm, Farnley bringing up the rear, a lifeless pigeon dangling from his left hand.

"Lucien!" Lady Penelope cried, running down the remainder of the stairs before skidding to a halt not a foot in front of the grinning pair. Pansy scurried past her to greet Farnley with an awkward curtsy, for she knew her husband, in his new exalted role of butler, was a stickler for propriety.

"Good morning, sweetheart," Lucien said, opening his arms to Penelope as she stood, catching her breath. "This is quite a greeting."

"You're all right! I thought you were dead, but you're all right!" Lady Penelope exclaimed, overjoyed. She was about to launch herself into his arms when a strange expression entered her eyes and the wide smile she had been wearing melted into a fearsome frown.

"You're all right," she repeated dully. "I thought you were dead, but you're all right. You're even happy, smiling." Her eyes narrowed into angry slits. *"Why, you—"* she gritted, and then she drew back her right arm just as her brothers had taught her, squeezed her fingers into a tight fist, and punched her beloved square in his beautiful, high-bridged Grecian nose!

"Packs quite a wallop, don't she?" Cyril was saying jovially a few minutes later as he reentered the drawing room, a cold wet cloth in his hand. "Here you go, Lucien. See if you can clean yourself up a bit now that the bleeding's stopped. You're enough to turn a man off his feed, and that's a fact."

Lucien lay sprawled in the French corner chair, his head leaning back over the edge, dabbing at his abused nose with his handerchief. "Thank you, Cyril. I guess I should have seen it coming, but she really took me by surprise. God, how I love that girl!"

"Now, there's something I thought I'd never hear," Philippos said from his chair across the room. "The last time I saw you, Lucien, you were expounding on the evils of matrimony. It rather depresses me to hear you waxing poetic about m'sister, you know, after all your fine words."

Turning his head to one side, the better to see the friend he had studiously avoided the night before, Lucien jibed, "Oh, really, Romeo? Then tell me, how ever did you tear yourself away from Lady Redfern? I'm sure she was still busily kissing your feet for offering for her Dorinda."

"I didn't offer for her," the Earl of Hawkedon corrected quietly, speaking into the opened neck of his dressing gown. "I thought about it right enough, but the more I saw of her, the more I realized that we just wouldn't suit."

"Oh?" Lucien commented, rising to a sitting position as Cosmo and Cyril hovered over him like mother birds fretting over one of their fledgling hatchlings. "I'm done spilling my claret all over the place, boys, so I think you can relax now. How so, Philip?"

Philippos's youthful features flushed hotly as he admitted, "She's just too ordinary."

"Ordinary? Lord, Philip, the woman's a known beauty. A diamond of the first water from all accounts. How could you call her ordinary?"

Spreading his hands wide, Philippos answered, "Think about it a minute, Lucien. St. John, Betancourt, Mannering—they all married such interesting women. Different— if you know what I mean. You know what Dorinda likes most? *Embroidery!* I've got three pair of slippers upstairs in my luggage now, every last one of them sporting pink birds on the toes, thanks to her. I tell you, I was thoroughly depressed until Cosmo came to take me away."

Leighton gingerly touched his tender nose, his most recent reminder of just how *different* Lady Penelope was. "I think I understand, Philip, and strangely enough, I agree with you. Now, how do you suppose I should go about approaching your sister? I'd hate to think I must first arm myself before I apologize to her. Where is she, anyway?"

Cosmo was only too happy to supply the answer. "She's off on Nemesis. She went pelting out of the stable yard a few minutes ago, after tearing a strip off Papa's hide. You should have heard her. It was wonderful!"

" 'When Greeks joined Greeks then was the tug of war,' Lee," Aunt Lucinda pointed out from her seat in the griffin-headed chair. She had joined the men after rushing through her morning toilette, which explained why her usual, overly ornate look today almost bordered on the—perish the thought—mundane.

"I thought she was going to stuff that pigeon straight in Papa's jaws when he tried to bamboozle her with that story of how he and Lucien went out hunting with dueling pistols," Philippos said, laughing as he remembered his father's shocked expression when Lady Penelope cut off his explanation with a single naughty word and then stomped back up the staircase, Doreen, Aunt Lucinda, and Pansy (who wasn't quite sure if she should be punishing Farnley, but who decided to follow the other ladies' lead) in her wake.

"We both deloped," Lucien explained yet again, for the twins had nearly fallen over themselves in unholy glee the first time they had heard the story and were now urging him to repeat it. "It was the strangest thing, really. We turned at the count of ten, both of us pointing our pistols at the other—although I had already decided to fire mine into the air and take my punishment like a man—when one of the grooms must have slammed the stable door, startling a dozen or so pigeons that had been asleep on the roof."

"Yes, yes," Cyril prodded, holding his sides as he chortled with mirth. "Tell us about the pigeon."

"Be patient, halfling, I'm getting to it. Just as I fired my pistol into the sky, your father turned toward the stable, took careful aim by steadying his pistol against his left forearm, and downed one of the pigeons on the wing, neat as you please. He was quite proud of himself and taking no pains to hide the fact, saying something about this being the first time he'd ever hit anything in a duel. Quite a man, you know, the Marquess. We shook hands, talked a bit about, er, this and that, and then he invited me in to share his breakfast."

"So tell us," Cosmo said consideringly, "now that you didn't duel, does this mean that Papa's going to make you marry Penny?"

"I don't think so," Cyril put in, wiping his streaming eyes. "It don't seem fair, somehow, after all he's already been through, to still end up saddled with a wife."

For once Aunt Lucinda lost patience with her beloved nephew. " 'Brain him with a lady's fan,' Shakespeare," she suggested, sighing.

Rising to his feet, Lucien turned to look at the twins— Cosmo, who liked the Earl well enough, but who still worried about the man's dubious influence on his dear sister; and Cyril, who found it hard to believe that anyone would want to marry a hey-go-mad girl who climbed down wells and put frogs in people's beds (even if she was a great gun)—and said quite seriously, "I love Penny with all my heart, and if she'll still have me, yes, I want to marry her. I appreciate having your father's blessing, but I'd marry her without it—or yours. Do you understand now?"

"To each his own, I guess," Cyril allowed, losing interest in the subject as his stomach set up a protest at having been neglected. "Come on, brother, I imagine there's no more sport to be had here, now that Lucien's getting all soft and sticky on us. Let's see if Papa's ate up all the kippers."

"You don't like kippers, you idiot," Cosmo reminded his brother, already following him out of the room.

"So what? I can't see why you're complaining," Cyril answered reasonably. "It'll leave all the more of the smelly things for you."

Once the twins were gone, Philippos rose and held out his hand to Lucien. "Welcome to the family, friend," he offered with a rueful shake of his head. "Much as I hate to say this, else you might think you should call *me* out, I believe you'll fit in quite nicely."

"Thank you, Philip, but you may be a bit premature," Lucien said, returning the gesture, and the two shook hands. "We'll have to hold off on the congratulations until I can ferret out my blushing bride—*and* until I can talk her out of murdering me for being so inconsiderate as not to die out there behind the stables like someone out of a Penny Press novel. I only wish—"

" ' 'A man must keep his mouth open a long while before a roast pigeon flies into it,'—" Aunt Lucinda said concerning wishes, before she stopped, unable for once to remember the source of a quote, her hands flying to her rouged cheeks in horror. " 'O shame! where is thy blush?' Shakespeare,'' she lamented before dashing from the room to search out the author amongst her vast store of books.

Philippos watched after her, a delighted smile on his face. "See what I mean, Lucien? I want someone like that: *different.* Do you think Aunt Lucinda has any more nieces hidden away besides Penny? Perhaps I shall follow her and ask. Good luck to you with m'sister and—oh, by the by, keep your guard up, for she's just as handy with her left as with her right!''

Lucien found Lady Penelope just where he had supposed he would, coming up behind her as she sat beneath the fading apple tree, Nemesis grazing nearby. Tying Hades's reins to a low-hanging branch some distance away, he picked his way carefully across the fallen leaves and sat down beside her, so that together they stared down the hill at the field where they had first met.

Neither of them spoke as the minutes passed by, until at last Lady Penelope, still without looking at him, challenged, "Well, are you just going to sit there like a statue? Aren't you going to say anything?''

"You have a good right hand,'' he congratulated her, adding, "although I think you'd get more power if you stood further front on your toes as you moved through the punch.''

Lady Penelope turned her head sharply to glare at him. "That's it? That's it! That's all you have to say?'' She jumped to her feet, angrily brushing away the leaves that clung to the seat of her riding habit. "I don't believe it!'' she announced to the birds and the trees—for her head was raised and she seemed to be speaking to the world in general. *"Do you believe it?* The man goes out to fight a duel with my father, and he comes back with a *pigeon!* And *he* wasn't even the one to shoot it! I've never been so humiliated in my entire life!''

Lucien rose slowly to his feet, enjoying the sight of his beloved in a rage, her unbound hair blowing about in the breeze as her entire small body quivered with indignation. "I told them you'd be angry I wasn't killed, but they didn't believe me,'' he said, trying to keep the laughter out of his voice. "I tried to step in front of your father's pistol, but as I have yet to learn how to fly, it was to no avail. Alas," he sighed, pretending deep despair, "it looks as if we'll have to be married after all."

Lady Penelope lowered her head, her full bottom lip thrust out sullenly. "Last night you said you loved me, yet you still went out this morning thinking you were to fight a duel. I don't think I'll ever understand you. I wish—"

" 'A man must keep his mouth open a long while before a roast pigeon flies into it,' " Lucien said as Lady Penelope's voice trailed away.

"That's very funny, in a strange sort of way. Who said it?" Lady Penelope still refused to look at him, but Lucien could tell that she was beginning to soften toward him, for her left shoulder had begun to shift closer to his, and her head was tilted in his direction.

"Aunt Lucinda, although the exact source seems to have slipped her mind. I've always wondered how she keeps all those bits and pieces of information in her head. It's almost comforting to know she has an occasional lapse. Oh, by the way, I meant what I said last night, my dear pugilist. I do love you. Very much."

"Then—then why did you still insist upon fighting the duel?" she asked, her shoulder now making a slight, burning contact with his chest.

Daring to take advantage of the unspoken invitation, Lucien slipped his arms around her waist and turned her about to face him. "That's a very long story, and one your father has advised me to tell you some rainy night when we are very, very old. Suffice it to say it had something to do with that ridiculous honor you view with such disdain."

"Oh," she returned in a small voice. "I guess I can agree to that, although I don't understand it. Er, please continue," she stammered, bemused by his closeness, the fresh scent of him reminding her of their heated embraces of the night just past.

"Gladly. If I promise to love you with all my heart forever and evermore, my pet, do you think we could forget everything that's happened and begin again? I have your father's permission to seek your hand in form. I'll go down on one knee, if you feel it necessary.''

Lady Penelope smiled up at him saucily through her long eyelashes, her anger completely dissipated. ''I think, considering all that has happened—for no matter what you say, I shall *never* forget last night—that we have progressed beyond such formality, don't you?''

Bending his knees, Lucien drew her slowly down to the ground beside him, holding her to his chest as his head lowered to within inches of her own. ''Why, Lady Penelope, you're such a scamp! Whatever do you mean?''

The scamp, her emerald eyes shining with love, reached a hand around his neck, pulling him down to her, and proceeded to show him *precisely* what she meant.

The Timeless Romances
of *New York Times* Bestselling Author

JOHANNA
LINDSEY

SECRET FIRE 75087-2/$4.50 US/$5.95 Can
From the tempestuous passion at their first meeting, theirs was
a fever that carried them to the power of undeniable love.

HEARTS AFLAME 89982-5/$3.95 US/$5.75 Can
Enemies in an age of war, they were lovers in passion's timeless
battle.

A HEART SO WILD 75084-8/$3.95 US/$5.75 Can
Searching for her father in Indian territory, Courtney put her
faith in Chandos—little dreaming of the dark secret that
burned in his soul or the fires that he would ignite in her.

WHEN LOVE AWAITS 89739-3/$3.95 US/$5.50 Can
The terrible demands of past hatreds and misunderstandings
would tear Leonie and Rolfe apart again and again—until they
learned the truth that only love can bring!

LOVE ONLY ONCE 89953-1/$3.95 US/$5.50 Can
TENDER IS THE STORM 89693-1/$3.95 US/$5.50 Can
BRAVE THE WILD WIND 89284-7/$3.95 US/$5.50 Can
A GENTLE FEUDING 87155-6/$3.95 US/$5.50 Can
HEART OF THUNDER 85118-0/$3.95 US/$4.75 Can
SO SPEAKS THE HEART 81471-4/$3.95 US/$4.75 Can
GLORIOUS ANGEL 84947-X/$3.95 US/$4.95 Can
PARADISE WILD 77651-0/$3.95 US/$5.50 Can
FIRES OF WINTER 75747-8/$3.95 US/$4.95 Can
A PIRATE'S LOVE 40048-0/$3.95 US/$4.95 Can
CAPTIVE BRIDE 01697-4/$3.95 US/$4.95 Can

AVON BOOKS

Lindsey 6/88